RUN FOR YOUR LIFE!

Betty Swinford

Moore Books

PO Box 324
Somerville, IN 47683

Run for Your Life!

Second Printing, September 2000

Cover artist: Jeannette Haley
PO Box 332
New Plymouth, ID 83655

Printed By: Old Paths Tract Society
Route 2, Box 43
Shoals, IN 47581

ISBN 1-891635-15-8

SECRETS

Fists hammered at the door, hard and demanding. Ten of those sitting at the table drinking tea, rose and scurried away like frightened mice. Six fled up the stairs, where they slid aside a wall panel and hurried within. Seconds later the panel was back in place and they were huddling together for safety. They scarcely breathed. No one moved.

Without a word, the remaining four downstairs moved aside the table, scooped up the rug and opened a trap door. Silently, two women and two men dove down into the darkness. Just as quickly, Franz Bedke and his mother replaced the rug and the table. Giving each other quick, anxious looks, Franz nodded to his father, who was waiting by the front door.

Yet, even as Hermann Bedke twisted the doorknob, Franz gazed frantically around the room. Was everything in place? Had each Jew taken with him his cup and saucer? This was very important, for nothing must be left to chance.

"Open up!" a voice thundered.

Adolf Hitler's reign of terror had now reached every corner of Germany. Year by year it had grown worse. The feared SS were ever on the prowl, looking for Jews. When they were found, they were immediately sent away, never to be heard of again. It appeared that Hitler had two main goals: one was to rule the world, and the other was to exterminate every living Jew.

Already, Jewish businesses had been destroyed. At first it was the word *Juden* smeared on storefronts. Then it was shattered glass, burning and destruction. Now their only hope lay with sympathetic Germans who were willing to risk their own lives to save them.

With a deep, shuddering breath, Hermann Bedke opened the door. He had known that their home was under suspicion but had prayed that this night would never come. To be arrested for concealing Jews meant death or imprisonment or both.

Three German soldiers in gray uniforms and bucket helmets stomped inside without a word. Their rifles were drawn as if expecting trouble. They raced from room to room, their faces dark and angry. They thumped the stairsteps, tapped the walls, and searched for any secret area where one might hide Jews.

"Where are the Jews?" one of the soldiers demanded angrily.

Franz's father frowned. "Jews? What Jews are you talking about?"

His reply was a slap in the face that staggered Mr. Bedke for a moment.

One of the soldiers was coming back downstairs. His boot heels sounded hollow and ominous on the steps. "Two bedrooms," he reported in defeat. "Both empty."

Franz stood rooted to the floor. He was a tall youth, five foot eight. His skin was fair, his eyes as blue as the sky, and he had a shock of blond hair that tended to fall over the left side of his forehead. He was just what Hitler loved, a true Aryan.

The first soldier pointed a long, accusing finger in Mr. Bedke's face. "Herr Bedke, your home is under suspicion! We know you are hiding Jews, and when we find them you will wish you had never been born!"

They left the house in a fit of rage, their boots making soft prints in the new snow. No lampposts were burning because of the blackout, and the three shadows melted away into the night.

The Bedke family sat down heavily at the table once more. It had been very close. If they had not been so diligent in performing drills, they might have been caught. Franz figured that it had taken the Jews no more than thirty seconds to pull a disappearing act.

Franz's mother poured more tea and set out a plate of fresh pastries. "I made these for all of us," she said, "but it's too dangerous for anymore movement in the house tonight!"

"I feel so badly for them," Mr. Bedke murmured, sighing. "Always hiding. Afraid. And the basement is so cold and damp."

Franz frowned at his plate. "They have blankets." Did his growing resentment show up in his words? He hoped not. And he didn't want to feel this resentment. Why, he loved the Jewish people! But it was hard for him too. Never being able to let a friend inside the house. Always on the alert. Always afraid.

His father's hand was trembling as he reached for a pastry. "We have to talk."

Franz saw his mother's blue eyes cloud over. How difficult it must be for her, struggling to supply food for the ten others in the home. Fighting the constant fear that surrounded them all.

Hermann Bedke sighed deeply. "Ruth," he said, addressing his wife, "Franz, you both know that we are now in constant danger of discovery." He sighed again, drank some tea, broke off a corner of the pastry. "I've thought about this for some time, and I have a plan that can mean freedom for all of us."

Franz tensed. Head down, he continued to stare at his plate.

"There are new connections," Mr. Bedke went on slowly, "ways to smuggle our Jews to safety." At this bit of news, both Franz and his mother sat forward eagerly. "The first link in this connection is a man, Josef Klotz. He waits for a dark rainy night, comes along on a bicycle and gives one Jew false identification papers. Then he puts him on the back of his bicycle and rides away into the night."

Ruth Bedke appeared puzzled. "Where does he take them?"

Hermann shook his head. "That's something we don't know. Each link in this connection knows only of one link. It's safer that way. What we do know is that each Jew will be smuggled to a safe place until this wretched war is over. Some will be sent to relatives in other countries, some to Palestine or perhaps to Switzerland. The point is, now we have the opportunity to save those we have taken in."

Franz was about to breathe a sigh of relief when his father shattered his hopes.

"But if we stay here in Germany, Jews will continue to come to us and eventually we'll all be caught. That's why I'm going to move our family to Poland."

"Poland!" Franz cried in disbelief. "Dad, no!"

"It's the only safe way for all of us, Franz. When the war is over—and it surely can't last much longer—then we'll move back to Germany."

Ruth Bedke fingered her uneaten pastry. "How many Jews will die if we leave?"

Hermann was growing desperate. "Ruth, we are under suspicion! If we stay and take in more Jews, then we all die! Don't you see?" There was an urgency in his eyes. "If we don't move quickly, there may be heavy travel restrictions. And because we already speak Polish, we should be able to make the move smoothly."

Franz's heart was thundering. His thoughts were a runaway train in danger of derailment. To leave his friends . . . his home. . . . If the Jews had never come here, they wouldn't have to leave!

"I don't want this either, but there is no other way." Mr. Bedke sighed deeply. "I promise we'll come home when this is over."

With heavy heart Franz gazed from his father's angular face, to his gentle gray eyes, to his thatch of brown hair. Leaving his pastry uneaten, he trudged up to his room. On the other side of the wall in the secret room someone snored softly.

Franz tried to pray, to place himself in the position of the Jews. It would be awful, hiding in darkness like animals. Ducking every time you passed a window during the day. Running. Always afraid of discovery. Always alert to unseen danger.

But the bitterness and resentment persisted. And try though he did not to hate Adolf Hitler, it was very hard.

"Lord Jesus, I know the Bible says You died for everyone, but . . . *Hitler?*" Franz asked, putting his thoughts into words.

Still on his knees, he told himself that not all the Nazis were evil. Take that soldier who had met the Jewish boy Bernard that day. He could have shot him on the spot, or hauled him away to some prison camp. Instead, he had smiled and said that he had a son like him at home. Bernard had stood paralyzed until the soldier had patted him on the shoulder, then turned and walked out of sight.

Franz had heard what the soldier said, and he knew that the next one might not be so kind. Since Bernard's parents had both been killed, Franz brought the boy home with him. Bernard was one of the first to be hidden in the Bedke home.

A twisted smile touched Franz's lips. Sure, it had been almost fun then. Challenging because it was dangerous and adventurous. But then others had drifted in and Franz's life had been completely disrupted. That was when the resentment began to build.

"It's hard to cope with, God," Franz prayed. "I mean, Jews are just people like everyone else, so why does Hitler hate them and teach others to hate them and kill them?"

Now, of course, every Jew had to wear a yellow Star of David to identify himself. And thousands disappeared every single day.

Franz finished praying and crept into bed, where he lay staring at the dark ceiling. He thought about the non-Jews who called them "Christ-killers," but he sure couldn't see that those people loved Jesus or lived for Him! Besides, he knew well that what nailed Jesus to the cross had been his own sins. His and the sins of the entire world; so the truth was, no one had killed Christ.

"What a crazy, mixed-up world it's become," he whispered to the silence. He shivered, knowing what was happening to Germany's Jews at that time. Still, why did *his* family have to be involved?

Franz was still wrestling within himself as sleep took him captive. Yes, he loved God's chosen people and felt sorry for them, but . . . to leave his home and friends? His country?

WARSAW, PolANd

Franz felt lost and lonely after their move to Poland. He told himself that he would make new friends, though his Polish definitely needed working on. And now he could invite other boys to the house! Secrecy and danger were now things of the past.

He sighed, remembering. The last Jew to be smuggled out had been Bernard. The shy, brown-eyed boy had been taken away on a dark rainy night. In spite of Franz's battle with resentment he and Bernard had grown close, and he was sorry to see the Jewish boy go. He had even suggested that Bernard might be taken along to Warsaw as part of the family.

"Franz," his father had explained patiently, "think about it. You and your mother are blond and blue-eyed, and I'm clearly non-Jewish. Bernard has olive skin and black hair and brown eyes." He sighed. "Now who do you think would believe that Bernard is a member of our family?"

And so Bernard had passed from his life. The last Franz had seen of him was that black stormy night when he had hopped onto the back of Josef Klotz's bicycle and pedaled away into the darkness. By midnight Bernard would be safe in some distant farmhouse, where he would wait for another dark night, then taken to the next link of the smuggling ring.

In Warsaw, Mr. Bedke located an empty store that could be easily converted into a bakery. And by spring, 1939, it was open for business. He also found a house for his family in a middle income neighborhood. It had a large upstairs and basement that covered the entire underneath of the house. A spooky place, with a number of small rooms and narrow, dank passages.

Their money had been exchanged. Reichsmarks were now Polish zlotys, though some German money had been kept for future use.

"I miss my friends in Germany," Franz complained at supper one night. Idly he toyed with his sour cabbage. "And I don't understand why I can't contact them."

Hermann Bedke put down his fork and sipped some black coffee. "Surely you can't have forgotten the fact that we were under suspicion there? That we were forced to move to avoid imprisonment?"

Franz's mouth twisted. "What does that have to do with where we are now? The Germans can't get to us here."

A dark frown slid over his father's forehead. "Franz, the whole earth is in a frenzy right now. Hitler's desire is to rule the world! We don't know what the future may hold for us, even here in Poland! Anyway, I'm sorry, but it's better if your old friends don't know yet where we are."

"The Germans won't come here!" Franz argued almost under his breath.

His father shook his head. "There are rumors, son. And surely you see men on the streets talking about the possibility of war. People are afraid, Franz." He picked up his coffee cup but did not drink. "I prayed we would be safe in Poland, but there is something in the air."

Mrs. Bedke sighed loudly. "Also, Franz, you remember, in Germany, how people began to distrust one another? The same is beginning to happen around us here. And we've noticed that there is more animosity toward the Jewish people in Warsaw."

Franz remembered, all right, how friends began informing on friends. And neighbors began turning in Jews who had been friends all their lives.

"But, Dad!" Franz exclaimed doubtfully. "Poland isn't at war!"

Mr. Bedke put down his cup. "No. Not yet." He forced a smile. "Eat your supper, Franz."

Franz didn't want to believe this, not any of it. It was a bad dream, a nightmare!

Absently he cut into a pierogy and scooped a little more sour cream on top of it. When he was younger he had often watched his mother make pierogies. She would stuff small squares of dough with potatoes, then boil them like dumplings. Afterwards they were eaten with either sour cream or gravy. It was one of his favorite foods, though at the moment they seemed tasteless and cold.

War in Poland? Surely not. Maybe his father was wrong. Maybe it was all a mistake.

What was Hitler doing anyhow, following them around?

War

The day was warm and muggy, the end of August 1939. Four miles away in the Jewish sector of Warsaw, a boy by the name of Karl Rosenthal was hurrying home for the Sabbath. He was a handsome youth, with great, warm brown eyes and dark, curly hair. Sensitive and spiritual, Karl often thought that he might someday become a rabbi.

It was nearly sunset, so he rushed inside to bathe and dress for the Sabbath meal. The aroma of cooking food reached out to him, and he knew his mother had gone to market early to purchase provisions for tonight's supper. Chicken soup with matzoh balls bubbled on the stove, and there was the wonderful fragrance of fine white challah bread, a bread baked for holy days or Sabbath.

His sister Sonia had carefully polished the silver and placed candles on the table. Everything was ready. His father, Moishe Rosenthal, looked splendid in a dark suit. He was just wrapping his prayer shawl around his shoulders. Karl felt a surge of pride at being his son.

"Good Shabbat, Father."

"Good Shabbat," the man responded in his deep, pleasant voice. "Hurry along, son, the Sabbath is about to begin."

Within ten minutes the family had gathered around the table and the candles were lighted. Karl's yarmulke was perched on his black curls. This was a wonderful, spiritual time that never lost its magic for him.

His mother wove her hands through the candle flames and began to pray. "Blessed art thou, O Lord our God, King of the universe. . . ."

Her prayer included not only praise but blessing for her family, and thanks for all God had done for them.

Moishe Rosenthal's prayer shawl now covered his head and he added a prayer of his own, ending it with, "Blessed art thou, O Eternal!"

They sang together, a sad, haunting Jewish hymn, and each member of the family uttered a heartfelt, "Omaine!"

Karl smiled with satisfaction. He loved to hear his mother and father pray and he loved God's Word. The beauty and mystery of the Sabbath never lost its charm for Karl Rosenthal.

His father kissed the fringe of his prayer shawl. But he had one more thing to do, something that had become a part of their Sabbath. He laid his hands on Karl's head and prayed he would be like faithful Abraham. After that he blessed Sonia also, and prayed that she would become like Abraham's wife Sarah. And finally the last "Omaine" was uttered. The Sabbath was now well underway.

Karl's father was a bricklayer and, though many Jews were wealthy, the Rosenthals were not. They did enjoy all the normal things in life, though. A cobbler came once each year to measure their feet and make them new shoes, but Golda Rosenthal made their clothes, baked their bread and made certain there was food enough to see them through the winter months.

"Father," Karl began earnestly as they were walking to synagogue the following morning, "when Sabbath has ended, could we take some time to talk?"

Mr. Rosenthal's eyes twinkled. "Of course! You sound as if you have some weighty matters on your mind." He added mischievously, "Not girl trouble, I hope."

Karl blushed. "Nothing like that!" Though he did have to admit that the new girl across the street was pretty cute. "I just need to talk to you, that's all."

Moishe started to ruffle his son's hair before he remembered that Karl was too old now for such foolishness. "We'll have your talk, Karl," he promised. Then in a low, troubled voice, "God knows there is enough to talk about these days."

It was several days, however, before there was opportunity for the father-son talk. They walked away from the house and along a quiet street. Karl's sensitive nature detected some ominous feeling in the air today. And he noted men in groups here and there in earnest conversation. It didn't take a genius to pick up on words like "trouble" and "war" and "disaster."

There was even something different about Mr. Rosenthal today. Maybe he looked a little older. Grim. Worried.

Overhead, leaves were dancing in the wind. Winters were harsh in Poland, and soon the trees would stand dark and bare. The wind would howl like a thing gone mad and the ground would be covered with snow.

"Father," Karl began slowly, "I want to know exactly what is happening in Poland. I hear people saying that the Germans will attack us, that war is coming very soon. I think maybe I'm a little afraid, but I want to know the truth. I'm not a child anymore."

"Karl, we are all afraid." Moishe Rosenthal's gentle face remained the same, but he had stiffened a little. "Son, today, September 1, Germany has already bombed our country."

Karl stared at his father, his dark eyes widening in shock. "Father . . . *when?*"

His father's handsome face was more serious than Karl had ever seen it. For a long time the man did not reply. Then, hesitantly, "This morning, Karl. It began at five o'clock this morning."

Karl felt a shiver race down his spine. His scalp tingled. "Warsaw hasn't been bombed!"

"Not yet, Karl. Germany has hit western Poland." Mr. Rosenthal kept walking, head down, staring off toward the street.

"They will strike Warsaw; it's only a matter of time." Suddenly the man relaxed a little. "But, Karl, here we go, borrowing trouble! Maybe the Poles will be able to hold them off, stop the Germans!"

This news was heavy for a young teenager to carry, and Karl had the feeling that he would have to grow up in a hurry. "Hitler!" Karl hissed. "I spit on Hitler!" He spit. "Why does he want to conquer the world anyway?"

Mr. Rosenthal appeared thoughtful. "Karl, you've studied history. It's never changed. It seems there is always some evil man who wants one thing above all else. Power. Isn't that really what war is all about?"

"I guess so."

"But just remember this, Karl, not all Germans are bad. There are many wonderful people in Germany. There are even good German soldiers who hate what's happening. Not all of them have had their minds poisoned by Adolf Hitler. In their hearts they hate Nazism as much as we do."

"I guess so," Karl said again. He thought all this over as they walked along. "I hear people talking, Father. They say that Hitler is having the Jews killed."

Now Moishe looked grim. "Our people have gone through terrible times before and survived. We will also survive this." The man patted his pocket. "By the way, Karl, a letter came through from your uncle Nathan. You remember him? Of course you do.

"Anyway, your Uncle Nathan was kept hidden by some Germans by the name of Bedke. Because of them, my brother is now safe in Switzerland."

Karl nodded gloomily. "I'm glad Uncle Nathan is safe, but that doesn't help us much if the Germans take Poland and begin persecution here."

"It could help a whole lot, Karl. You see, the Bedkes are now in Warsaw."

"Really, Father?"

"Really," Moishe said, nodding. "And now we have had our talk, so it's time to turn back. Your mother will scold us both if we're late for supper."

Days crawled past. Everyone had their ears tuned to their radios for the latest news. Rumblings of war became more and more threatening. And suddenly, on September 8, it was announced that there would be no school.

At breakfast Karl grinned slyly. "I'm not exactly crushed about not having to go to school today. It just means that me and Jankele and the others can play soccer out in the street."

Almost before the words left his lips, however, there was a faraway humming sound. Karl and his sister Sonia raced outside to see what it was.

"Karl, look," Sonia said, pointing to the sky. "What are all those little black specks over there?"

Karl felt his body go rigid. Grabbing his sister's hand, he pulled her back inside the house. "Mother, the sky is filled with airplanes!"

Warsaw Is Bombed

Mrs. Rosenthal darted to the window to peer up at the sky. The low hum they had heard before rapidly turned into a loud droning sound. As she watched, puffs of smoke began to explode upwards as bombs dropped. The sounds they made were chilling and ominous.

Alarmed and stunned, she turned away. "Sonia, quickly, grab all the blankets you can carry and go to the basement! Karl, help me get some food together!"

They were just bolting down the basement steps when neighbors began streaming inside. These were people who had no basements and knew that the Rosenthals would welcome them. Most had nothing at all to contribute, they had left home in such a hurry. One had a baby in her arms.

Thirty-four people crowded into the basement. When men hurried home from work, the number grew to forty. Moishe Rosenthal's dark eyes scanned the group to be sure his wife and children were safe.

"Oy, oy," one woman groaned, clenching her hands, "such a day we should live in! Everything we have will be destroyed!"

Karl's father took quiet control of the situation. "We don't know that at all. What we do know is that the God of Abraham is with us."

His strong, confident voice brought a measure of calm to them all. But as the planes grew ever closer and the blasts of exploding bombs threatened to bring the house down upon them, women and children began to cry.

Karl could see the planes through a small basement window. Some were flying in a *V* formation. Others were coming in a straight line. The world was a gigantic bowl of dust, smoke, and flames.

"Karl," Mr. Rosenthal shouted above the sounds of bombing, "bring me the lamp!"

Wrenching himself away from the window, he got the naphtha lamp and tried to hold it steady while his father touched a match to the wick. In the dancing yellow flames their eyes met and Mr. Rosenthal smiled.

"Be brave, Karl."

"I am, Father."

With the soft golden light glowing in the darkness things seemed less frightening. Faces, though, were white and strained.

The baby was crying.

"Karl, did you or your mother think to bring water?"

Karl was back at the window, trying to see, feeling half paralyzed from what he saw. "No, Father. We only grabbed some food and blankets."

"Then we'll go for water when there's a letup in the bombing."

A spine-tingling explosion sent all of them cowering. Karl turned from the window quickly and Sonia pressed close to him for comfort. Awkwardly he patted her shoulder. That one had been much too close.

"It can't last forever," he assured her.

Five days later he wondered at his brave words. Bombs continued to fall. The wild chatter of artillery fire filled the air. Still the planes came, diving straight at the ground, dropping their bombs, then zooming again into the sky.

Whenever there was a lull, Karl and his father raced upstairs for buckets of water, then returned quickly to the cold shadows of the basement. On one excursion Mr. Rosenthal grabbed a radio and took it back down with him.

Oddly enough, after the third or fourth day, when they all realized the house was still standing, children entertained each other with games to try and make the time pass. Still, everyone's nerves were tense and there was fear upon every face.

On the eighth day the men turned sadly from the radio. Poland had surrendered. "We are under German rule," someone muttered sorrowfully. "The Eternal have mercy on us!"

The bombing stopped suddenly. After all the noise of the past few days, the stillness was eerie and strange. People crept from the basement and went to see what was left of their homes.

Karl and Sonia explored the house like detectives looking for clues.

"All the cups and saucers fell off the shelf and broke," Sonia announced to anyone who would listen.

"I guess we'll have to get new ones." Karl laughed a nervous laugh that broke in two. "Sonia, look out here!"

Sonia went to join her brother. The glass in every window was shattered. Across the street, once fine houses were now piles of flaming rubble. Everywhere they looked was fire and smoke. People walked on the street like zombies, unable to believe that all they had worked for was gone.

Tears slid down Sonia's face. "I can't believe our house is still standing!"

Woodenly, Karl turned from the window and began picking up the books that had fallen from the bookcase. Then he went to the kitchen to help his mother restore order.

Later, on a cool, sunny day in September, Karl went with his friend Jankele to watch the thousands of German soldiers marching through Warsaw. Along with them were too many Volkswagen Jeeps to count, too many tanks. They rolled down Marshalkowska Avenue, the enormous tanks making the ground tremble under the boys' feet.

Thousands of Poles had turned out to watch this awesome parade of invaders filling their land.

"Do you know what they called this invasion?" Jankele raised his voice so Karl could hear.

"What?" Grasping Jan's wrist, Karl pulled him back under a tree. Jankele was short and stocky and built like a box. Usually he had a merry twinkle in his eyes. But not today. The war had sobered everyone.

"They call it the *Blitzkrieg*, because it was over so fast."

"The *Lightning War*," Karl repeated wonderingly. "That's a good name for it. I still can't see why the Polish army could not hold off the Germans."

Jan's gaze swept the area. "And just look what they left behind. Everything is a mess. It will take a long time for them to clean up."

"Ha!" Karl scoffed. "The Germans will probably make the Poles clean it all up! You know how much they hate us."

Karl continued to examine the area. Chunk of concrete, splintered wood and broken glass were everywhere. Mountains and mountains of it.

"Karl?" Jankele said wistfully. "The Germans don't just hate the Gentile Poles, they hate the Polish Jews!"

"So what else is new?" Karl exclaimed wryly, "In case you haven't noticed, the Gentile Poles aren't exactly crazy about us either!"

Tromp . . . tromp . . . tromp . . . tromp. . . .

The goose-stepping German boots thudded the earth in perfect unison. The soldiers looked neither to the right nor the left but kept their eyes straight forward. Thousands . . . thousands. . . .

"What's going to happen now?" Jan asked softly.

Karl blew out his breath. "I guess we'll just have to wait and find out."

They didn't have to wait very long. Ration cards were passed out for food. Identification papers that carried their fingerprints and pictures must be upon a person at all times and could be demanded at a second's notice. It was a whole new way of life and Karl had a sinking feeling that the worst was yet to come.

"There are rumors," Karl heard a farmer telling another man on the street one day. "Our people are being systematically killed in Germany every single day. They are taken to labor camps and concentration camps and gas ch—" Seeing Karl listening in, he broke off and moved away.

Still, as time passed, life became more or less normal again. At least for the young people and the children. Sonia skipped rope with her friends and Karl got together with his friends for soccer. It didn't seem too bad so far. With the ration cards, there was enough food to live on. People could obtain potatoes, flour, sugar, turnips, bread, and onions. Once in a while they even enjoyed the luxury of cheese or kosher sausage.

But on November 23, while Karl was playing ball with some friends, Jankele appeared and pulled him out of the game.

"Karl, we have to talk!"

Karl tried to pull away. "Come on, Jan, join in the game with us."

"No, Karl, I have to tell you something."

Reluctantly Karl followed Jankele to the sidelines. He was sweating in spite of the chilly weather. "You should have joined us, Jan, it was a great game."

Jankele pulled Karl over to the steps of a bombed-out house and brushed aside a skiff of snow to sit down. "This is serious!"

Karl grinned. "So was the game! Anyway, Jan, you're too serious these days."

"Just listen!" Jan hissed. "You act like the war never even happened and-"

Karl sighed impatiently. "Jan, all these houses will be built back someday. All our windows have been replaced and I see building going on around here all the time."

Jankele shook his head sadly. "You just don't get it, do you?"

Karl gave his childhood friend a sharp look. "What are you talking about?"

Jan had never looked so serious. "I'm talking about the fact that all Jews now have to wear armbands with the Star of David so we can be recognized!"

Karl stared in disbelief. His throat felt dry. "Armbands?" he repeated.

Jan nodded. "That's what they made the Jews do in Germany. Only in Germany they had to wear yellow Stars of David. Here in Poland it's armbands. White with a blue Star." Jankele's black eyes were grim and frightened. "Karl, we can be singled out anywhere. Anytime. We'll never be able to hide our identity."

"Then if things get really bad. . . ."

"And, Karl," Jankele broke in, "if a Jew is stopped on the street, even if he has papers but isn't wearing his armband, he'll be shot on the spot!"

Someone's at the Door

The Bedkes' home had also survived the bombing, though many in their neighborhood had lost everything, even their clothes.

Most of the basement rooms beneath their house stood stark and empty, but the two larger rooms were crammed with food for the bitter winter ahead. Butter was sealed in large crocks, and there was a small mountain of root vegetables. Onions, turnips, beets, potatoes and carrots. There was also a supply of sour cabbage, flour, sugar, sausages and cheese. And so far the Germans had not raided their basement, though there had been a door-to-door search for radios.

"I knew it was coming," Hermann Bedke told Franz and his mother. "We must never let anyone know that there is a radio hidden beneath one of the steps."

Franz nodded and glanced toward the stairway. He was well aware that the Germans did not want the public to be able to hear the news. But at night, when the blackout curtains were drawn, he gathered with his parents to listen to what was going on in the world.

"Dad, what do you think is happening to the Polish Jews?" Franz was still fighting resentment over having to move to Warsaw because of the Jews, but he tried hard to hide that fact.

Mr. Bedke drew in a long, slow breath. "Son, that's something I try not to think about too much, though I certainly pray for them." He shook his head. "As long as Hitler remains in power no Jew in Europe is safe."

"I think it's rotten!" Franz burst out. He *did* think it was rotten. At the same time he was relieved that the Jews were no longer his personal problem.

His mother was sitting under the light, busy knitting him a warm sweater. Her golden hair was braided and lay in a soft coil at the back of her head. "This whole war is rotten, Franz. We just have to make sure that we don't become bitter and hateful. Remember that Jesus loves even Hitler and the brutal German soldiers too."

Franz stuffed his hands in his pockets. "I know that, Mother, it's just hard to believe." His eyes narrowed. "I suppose if we had stayed in Germany we'd be in prison by now."

"Yes, Franz," his father replied, nodding, "we would be in prison. And what Jews we would have been harboring would be dead. Actually, long before the soldiers came to our house looking for Jews, I saw them watching our home night after night. I never told you because I didn't want you to be worried."

Karl's mother seemed far away. "So we were under surveillance for a long time."

"A long time," Hermann Bedke said slowly.

Franz moved closer to the stove, where a fire crackled and snapped merrily. It was a cold, snowy night and clouds had turned the night dark very early. Great, heavy flakes were falling fast and white. So far Franz had made three trips to the cold, damp basement for buckets of coal for the greedy stove.

Mrs. Bedke's thoughts were still on her native Germany. "I'll be so thankful when this war ends and we can go back home."

"So will I," Franz agreed. "After all, Hitler won't be in power forever!"

His father reached for his worn Bible. The wind was a monster that roared around the house and moaned like a frightened child through the shuttered windows, so that the man had to raise his voice to be heard.

Before he could begin reading, though, another sound caught his attention. Ruth Bedke heard it, too, and lifted her head. "What was that?"

The sound came again, hard, insistent.

"It sounds like someone at the door," Franz said wonderingly, and had no idea that he was whispering.

Mr. Bedke laid aside the open Bible. "Maybe a shutter has come loose and is banging against the—" He didn't finish as the knock came a third time. "Stay here," he cautioned his family. "I'll see who it is."

Since everything was in blackout, he opened the door only a crack. There were wild tales around of the dreaded SS officers breaking into people's homes without warning. They were fearsome creatures in their black uniforms and red armbands with black swastikas. And their black caps with the skull and crossbones made them frightening figures indeed. Maybe they had come to rob the Bedkes of any gold or money they might have. And since movement at night was almost zero, when there was a knock at the door this time of night, people cringed in fear.

Franz heard a murmur of voices and heard his father say, "Come inside quickly!"

Mrs. Bedke half rose from her chair. Franz felt his arms go limp at his sides. Before them stood a man and a woman. Their coats and hats were covered with snow and there was terror in their eyes. No one had to tell Franz and his mother that their visitors were Jews.

"Welcome," Hermann Bedke was saying gently.

Ruth Bedke rushed to take their hats and coats. "Franz, put on water for tea."

"We're so sorry," the man stammered. "Things are getting very bad for us now in Warsaw. We had to get away!"

From the kitchen Franz heard his father say, "No need to apologize," and he was always amazed at the way his dad made Jews feel like old friends.

As for Franz himself, his heart had plowed a furrow all the way to his shoes. This was absolutely crazy! A nightmare! Here they were in Poland and it was happening all over again!

"But, God, I love the Jewish people!" Franz cried silently. "They're *Your* people! I don't want to feel this way!"

He went back into the living room to see the strangers warming themselves at the stove. Yeah, they were Jews, all right. Not even false identification papers could ever help them! Dark hair and eyes, Roman noses, olive skin, they were Jews all the way.

Only after Mrs. Bedke brought in cherry tarts and cups of steaming tea and they all sat down to talk did the newcomers relax.

"Now then," Mr. Bedke smiled, "how did you know to come to us?"

"I have a cousin in Germany." The man waved his hand. "At least, he *used* to be in Germany. Thanks to you, he is now safe in Switzerland. He managed to get word to us that you had moved to Warsaw and that you would help us."

"Of course we'll help you," Franz's father promised. "Tonight you'll sleep in one of the upstairs bedrooms and, tomorrow . . . well, I hope you're good with a saw and hammer, because we'll have to start working on a secret room."

Franz kept his head down. He was buried in thought. So moving to Poland hadn't done any good after all, except to keep them all out of prison a little longer.

"Now I want you to think," Hermann said suddenly. "Did anyone see you come here?"

"No one. We were very careful not to be seen."

Mrs. Bedke offered them more tea. "You haven't told us your names," she reminded them.

The man put down his cup and grasped his wife's cold hand. "My name is Moses Lipman. This is my wife Johanna. We're grateful to you for taking us in. We hope it won't be for long."

"We all hope the war will be over soon. Meanwhile," Hermann assured them, "we are your friends. However, there are certain things you have to be aware of. For instance, only at night will you be really free to move about the house. During the day, if you pass a window, you must crawl. Even flushing the toilet when we are away would be a dead giveaway. And there will be drills to see how quickly you can hide."

Moses looked grim. "We've never had to hide before, but we'll learn."

"It will get easier after we've created a secret room. But any time you must dive into it, you must be sure to take with you whatever you had before. A cup and saucer, anything. Never leave traces of your presence in the house." Mr. Bedke's grin was a little lopsided. "We must have full cooperation at all times for all our sakes."

Moses managed a tight smile. "You have our word on it."

Franz also knew the routine, having lived through it all before. Still, he shuddered at the thought of reliving it. Always on the alert. Always afraid that soldiers would come, breaking down doors, looking for Jews. Never bringing home a friend. Guarding his words, his lips.

Johanna Lipman looked small and scared, and Franz felt compassion for her in spite of himself. Only why couldn't they have gone somewhere else for protection? Why did it have it be *their* house?

The Ghetto

So far, Karl Rosenthal and his parents were all right. Their identification papers were in order and ration cards gave them enough to eat. White armbands with blue stars marked every Jew in Poland. Still they were being shot to death on the streets and many were mysteriously disappearing. It was 1940.

The smell of smoke and charred wood hung heavy on the damp air. The Germans had targeted the Jewish neighborhood heavily, reducing their homes to rubble. People roamed the streets in a haze of unbelief.

"What's going to happen, Father?" Karl inquired anxiously. "It doesn't feel safe anywhere."

Morning prayers had just ended and they were at the breakfast table. Golda Rosenthal was putting potato pancakes on Karl's plate.

"That's because it *isn't* safe," Moishe Rosenthal told his son. "And Jewish shops are under terrible persecution."

Karl flinched, remembering the last time he had ventured out of his neighborhood. Ugly words and the Star of David marked Jewish storefronts. Precious food had been flung out onto the sidewalks and scattered into the streets. In other businesses, wares were slashed and torn apart. Shards of glass were everywhere.

Sonia spoke for the first time. "The Poles are turning against us too."

Mr. Rosenthal threw back his head and laughed. "And who ever said that we were their favorite people anyway?"

Karl wondered how his father could laugh at a time like this. With all the persecution, how could there be anything to laugh about ever again?

Minutes later there was a hammering at the door. Before anyone could answer, a heavy boot kicked open the door, breaking the lock. Two gray-uniformed soldiers stomped into the house. Karl's father was instantly on his feet and about to protest such violence. An instant later he changed his mind and said nothing. Protesting anything the Germans might do could mean death to both him and his family.

He bit back his anger. "How can I help you?"

The soldiers glared at him in hatred. Their uniforms were spotless, their high black boots spit-polished and shining. Sidearms hung at their waists. Over their shoulders they carried rifles with bayonets. Outside at the curb a green army lorry waited, motor idling.

"Moishe Rosenthal?" one of the men demanded angrily.

Karl stood in the background, frowning. Why did the Germans always have to sound to angry?

"I am Moishe Rosenthal," his father replied calmly.

"You are a bricklayer."

The soldier made it sound like an accusation, but Moishe only nodded. "That's right."

"Report for work at four a.m. sharp."

No explanation was given, and after a few more remarks the soldiers turned abruptly and were gone. The doors to the motor lorry slammed and the vehicle rumbled away.

Karl's mother relaxed a little. "They didn't even say why you have to report to them for work."

Moishe was not laughing now. Sitting back down at the table he picked up his coffee cup. "I know why," he said grimly. "If only the Almighty had seen fit for us to obtain false identification papers! Now it's too late."

"Too late for what?" Sonia questioned.

Golda Rosenthal poured him more coffee and he stirred in some milk. "They're going to shut us in," he whispered.

Karl's heart began thudding insanely. Fear seized him. "You mean . . . you don't mean *a . . . ghetto?*"

Moishe closed his eyes to hide his pain and humiliation. "Yes, a ghetto. That's what this is all about. We are to begin building the wall."

"But, Father, *why?*" Sonia wailed.

"Ah, child, who can tell?" Mr. Rosenthal sighed.

Karl scrambled out of bed early next morning. He had to see for himself if the Germans really were going to shut in the Jewish population. If so, what would they do for food? The nearby shops would quickly run out of things.

Jankele found him sitting forlornly on the steps of a bombed-out house. A German flag flew proudly not far away, telling the world that it had conquered Poland. The blood-red banner seemed to float on the summer air. In the center was a great white circle and inside the circle was the hated black swastika.

Jankele peered at it angrily. "I hate that flag!" he announced bitterly. "And I hate the swastika!"

"All the Poles hate it," Karl agreed. "But you know what, Jan? A lot of the Poles are working for the Germans now, and they would turn us in for a zloty!" He shrugged. "But I guess they want to stay on the good side of the Germans."

Jankele rolled his eyes. "I suppose." Suddenly he grabbed Karl's arm. "Look!"

Karl gasped and stood for a better look. "There it comes, Jan, the wall is going up."

The Rosenthal home was very close to the tall gray wall, so the boys could watch what was happening. It wasn't even a good wall but was thrown together quickly. As the boys continued to watch, they saw with horror that pieces of broken glass were being embedded on top of the wall.

Karl clenched his teeth. "So much for anyone trying to climb over."

Jan's eyes were filled with anger. "We're going to be prisoners, Karl."

"And it's *our* country!" Karl cried bitterly.

By suppertime Karl had some idea of how things were going to change. The family sat down to boiled potatoes and watery gravy. He stared at the food mournfully.

"We have to get used to it," his father announced, "because things are going to get a lot worse." He sighed and scratched his chin. "Countries are toppling like dominoes. Poland, Norway, Denmark, Belgium, Holland, France. . . ."

"Isn't that enough?" Karl muttered. "What does Hitler want anyway?"

Moishe pressed his lips into a fine line. "He wants more."

"He's going to starve us," Sonia whimpered.

Karl bit his lip. "No, he's not! I'll find a way out of the ghetto to get food, just you wait and see!"

His father finished the potatoes hurriedly and left the table. "I have to think about this," he told his family, and went off to be alone.

Karl left too. It was minutes before curfew and he wanted to share something with Jankele. Already, he had it planned in his mind. It was all about that bombed-out house right next to the new wall. He nodded to himself. It was the perfect place to dig a tunnel under the wall so they could crawl out for food. Since there was a curfew, the streets would be deserted early. He and Jan would steal down there and begin working. It would be a snap!

Then they could remove their armbands from time to time and crawl out for food for their families.

"We'll have to be careful, though," he told himself as he walked along. "We'll have to have some boards to cover the hole from the other side of the wall, but. . . ."

Already, things were bad. Garbage had not been picked up and the streets reeked with rotten bits of food. Rats scurried around, nosing into garbage, looking for treats. Houses were shattered, many burned to the ground.

Then he was at Jankele's home, where he quickly stopped, staring at the sight before him. What was going on here anyhow? Lifting his voice, he yelled, "Hey, what do you think you're doing?"

This was insane! People were racing in and out of Jan's house with pieces of furniture, food, anything they could carry.

Those coming out of the house gave him a curious look, then went on with their looting.

Hot anger coursed through Karl's veins. "Stop! This is my friend's home!"

A swarthy-skinned old man paused for only a moment. "Maybe it *was* your friend's home, but it's not his now!"

"What's going on? What happened?" Karl slumped down on the bottom step. His mouth went dry and his heart was a machine gun. "Where are they?"

The old man spread his arms wide. "Gone, just like hundreds of others." He flicked his fingers at Karl. "You'd better go home or you'll be next."

No! The word screamed through Karl's mind. The Germans couldn't have taken Jankele and his family!

Karl despised the looters. They appeared almost happy when other Jews disappeared so they could steal their possessions. His feet felt like lead as he started back home.

"It's not fair, God. We never did anything to deserve this."

Gone. Jankele was gone. His childhood friend. He could hardly believe it.

He must hurry. Perhaps his family would be the next to disappear. Suddenly all his plans to dig the tunnel meant nothing. He started to break into a run when a hand came down on his shoulder. All the blood drained from his head and he was dizzy and weak. Sick and terrified. Now they had him too. Was it the dreaded SS or soldiers like the one who had broken into their home yesterday? He was afraid to look.

"It's only me, Karl. It's all right."

Karl turned slowly, like one in a dream. He was facing a man with a flowing gray-streaked beard. The long black coat and black hat and side curls marked him for a rabbi.

"Such a frightened boy you are, Karl!" The rabbi sounded surprised and comforting, too, somehow. "I know your friend and his family have been taken. So it is time to remember that the God of Abraham, Isaac, and Jacob is still in charge, true? Of course, true." His eyes were kind and he tugged gently at his beard. "So, Karl, keep your eyes upon the Eternal, eh? Such bad times we live in, but God still lives, no? So when the world is upside down, then we Jews remember . . . *gam zeletauvo*. All things work for good."

Karl's legs were still weak. "Thank you, Rabbi Dobschiner."

Like a wispy black phantom, the rabbi turned and disappeared in the shadows. His long black coat flapped around his thin body like the tattered wings of a wounded crow.

Karl tried valiantly to follow the rabbi's advice, but his heart was a chunk of lead. Jankele was gone. Only this morning they had watched together as the wall began to be erected.

It was curfew and Karl was surrounded by vengeful shadows. An army lorry was lumbering down the street. To be caught out after curfew meant death!

He ducked behind the rubble of a bombed-out building. There, breathless and frightened, he waited for the vehicle to pass and then dashed from his hiding place. He prayed fervently that he would not run headlong into the arms of a soldier or some SS officer.

"Karl!" His mother had been waiting anxiously at the door, and when she saw him dash up the steps, quickly pulled it open. "Karl, you must never go out this late! Never!"

"They've taken Jan and his family!" he blurted out.

His mother turned white at the words. His father, hearing what he said, entered the room with a cup of coffee in his hand.

"Are you sure?"

"It's true, Father! Jan and his parents are gone, and you should see the looters! They act like it's some kind of party."

Moishe Rosenthal took off his glasses and rubbed his eyes. "I've been thinking about all this for the past hour." His sigh was deep and ragged. "If we're to survive this war, there's only one thing to do: we have to get out of here while we still can."

SECRET ROOM

To cover the sounds of building, Ruth Bedke played the piano as loudly as possible. Her favorite instrument was the violin, but during this time she remained at the piano for hours on end. Often Franz stood beside her playing his saxophone. Anything to hide the sounds of sawing and hammering.

"Honestly, Mother," Franz told her one day, "I think every Jew that we hid in Germany had relatives or friends in Poland!"

The woman laughed. "They certainly know all about us and where to find us, all right!"

"Mother?" Franz hesitated. "I love the Jews and hate what's happening to them, but. . . ." He sighed and frowned. "Well, what about food and all?"

At this, Mrs. Bedke quickly sobered. She had detected the rumble of discontent in her son's voice. "With ten more people to care for, our food supply is dwindling very fast. But, Franz, as long as your father has the bakery, none of us is going to starve."

Yeah, well, he'd have to be blind not to see that the root vegetables were fast disappearing. He knew for a fact that there was only one barrel of sour cabbage left. The last of the cheese and sausage had been eaten weeks ago, and chicken was only a distant memory. Besides, the Bible stated clearly that man could not live by bread alone.

"The real problem," his mother admitted, "is that here in Poland we have no connections to smuggle these people to safety."

Franz wished in his heart that the Jews had never found them. That they had found other ways to survive without messing up his life all over again. He tossed his blond head to shake away the thought. That wasn't just or fair and he knew it. It was just. . . .

"Where could they go even if we did have connections?" he asked glumly. "Hitler's got just about all of Europe."

"Switzerland is free, if only we could get them there." The work upstairs stopped for while, so Ruth Bedke stopped playing and went to stare out the window. "You must be very careful, Franz. How you act. What you say. There is danger everywhere."

Franz felt that he was being forced to grow up too fast. Yes, he was pressing past childhood and into manhood, but were all his teen years going to be scattered to the winds? Everything was moving so fast. Hitler was sweeping Europe so rapidly that it boggled the mind. Franz felt as if he were trapped in a raging river from which there was no escape.

Mrs. Bedke touched his arm. "Let's go see the new room, Franz. I think they have it completed."

The secret room was on the other side of Franz's bedroom and the wall between them was thin. There was a secret panel in the bookcase. By removing the bottom shelf and sliding aside the panel, one could go through on his hands and knees, then simply replace the shelf and the panel. A pile of warm blankets waited in a corner for those times when the Jews must spend the night there.

Most of the time they slept downstairs, but in an emergency the secret room was always waiting for them. Six people could sleep there comfortably.

A second secret room in the dark basement would hide the other four in an emergency. They had constant drills to see how quickly the Jews could vanish into their hiding places. The last time they had made it in 56 seconds.

Ruth Bedke turned with satisfaction. "It should work well. Now, Franz, will you double check to see that the front door is locked, then call everyone to supper?"

He dove back down the stairs and checked the door. Several people were lounging in the living room. "Mother says supper's ready," he told them. Going to the door leading down into the basement, he called softly, "Jozef, Ingrid, everyone—supper's ready!"

Franz stared with disdain at the simple supper of black bread, boiled turnips and fried onions. Glancing around the table, he tried to feel compassion for these Jews who had lost it all just because of who they were. Then he thought of the wonderful supper they would enjoy if the Jews were not there.

He glanced over to his rucksack, waiting in silence, all packed and ready in case the SS ever broke into the house and they were arrested. It contained a change of clothing, matches, needle and thread, toothbrush and toothpaste, a small Bible, dried food, comb, and note pad and pencil. On top of the rucksack was his coat and cloth cap. Sewed into the lining of his coat were some German marks and some Polish zlotys. Just in case.

"We'll have dessert a little later," Mrs. Bedke said, smiling. "I managed to make something special."

"But first," Mr. Bedke suggested, "why not spend a little time reading God's Word? Are you in agreement?"

One elderly man nodded eagerly. "Such a time this is! We all need to hear what God has to say, eh?"

A few, though, appeared nervous and uncomfortable. Their anxiety deepened when Franz handed his father his Bible.

"Dad will read from the Old Testament," Franz explained. "It says the same thing your Bible says."

Jozef leaned forward with a twinkle in his eyes. "So, Frau Bedke, now you are blackmailing us poor helpless Jews! Oy! The Word of God for dessert, no?" He wiggled a finger at Franz. "And such a good Jewish boy you are that you know what our scriptures say? So you have been to Yeshiva school, eh? You are a rabbi, yes?"

Soft laughter filled the room. In a strange way they had become a family these past weeks. Even Franz could lay aside his resentment for a moment.

"You don't have to be a Jew or a rabbi to know the Old Testament!" Franz protested.

Jozef sobered. "Such a strange people you Christians are that you should love our Bible! What can it mean to you?" When Mr. Bedke would have answered, he held up a hand. "No, let us see whether our young rabbi knows the answer."

"We love the Old Testament; Franz said, "because the prophets pointed to what was going to happen."

Jozef was having a ball now. "Such as?" he pressed. "Exactly what did they say that it meant something to Goyim?"

Franz did not hesitate. "The most important thing they told us was about the coming Messiah. Even Moses, and—and Isaiah and Zechariah and others told us about the Saviour, Jesus. So of course we love your Bible and your prophets."

Jozef slowly edged back in his chair, astonished. "So you did not go to Yeshiva school after all." He waved a hand. "So go on, Herr Bedke, read, read."

All the Jews were nervous now. Some stared at their hands; others kept their eyes fixed upon the table. The name of Jesus made them uncomfortable.

Finally one elderly man spoke up, sounding very Jewish. "So, Jozef, so you asked for it! So next time don't ask so many questions, right? Of course right!"

Jozef looked sheepish and did not answer.

No one else said anything either, and Hermann Bedke began rustling the pages of the Bible. He stopped at the book of Joshua and began to read. At chapter 10 verse 25, he spoke slowly. " 'Fear not, nor be dismayed, be strong and of good courage; for thus shall the Lord do to all your enemies against whom you fight.' "

One of the men slapped his knee. "That was good, Herr Bedke, exactly what we needed."

"It's easy to forget the promises of God when the battle is raging," said another.

A number of "Omaines" floated around the dining table as they all agreed.

"But, Frau Bedke," Jozef said, smiling, "you did say that we have dessert tonight?"

A large platter of crisp, golden brown, sugary apricot dumplings were brought to the table, along with a pot of fresh coffee. An old bewhiskered Jew asked God's blessing upon the dessert in Yiddish. Because Yiddish was so much like German, the Bedkes could understand part of it.

"My, oy," a lady murmured, her eyes closed, "I will eat these in my mind when I am in the concentration camp!"

"Don't talk like that!" Ruth Bedke told her. "We must trust God and remember His promises!"

In the midst of the gaiety and chatter, a sharp rap sounded at the door. Heads lifted in alarm. Next instant, all the Jews had taken their plates and cups and were scattering silently to the secret rooms. Some fled upstairs, while others dove into the basement. While Mr. Bedke started for the door, Franz and his mother gazed about wildly to make certain all was in order.

Terror By Night

The blackout curtains kept every sliver of light inside the house. Outside, a brisk wind was blowing in the trees. Maybe it would rain. They hoped not.

Moishe Rosenthal looked tired and old. Gesturing toward chairs, he said, "Golda, sit down. Children, sit. It's time to make plans."

"What are we going to do, Papa?" Sonia used her childhood term for her father now. She shivered, unsure and afraid.

Sonia was blond with blue eyes, the only member of the family who would have passed for an Aryan . . . except for those identification papers she had to carry!

Karl stood for a moment longer, his hands gripped behind his back and trying very hard to look like a man.

Golda Rosenthal sat quietly with her hands laced in her lap.

Karl could see the fear in her eyes.

Moishe Rosenthal looked around the room. One wall was filled with his favorite books. "We have to leave," he said quietly. "Now, while there is still time."

"Leave?" Sonia echoed blankly. "What do you mean? Where would we go?"

The man pulled a crumpled letter from his pocket. "You remember, this letter from my brother Nathan came some time ago. He told me where we could go if ever we needed to hide. If we don't get away now, when the wall is finished it will be too late."

Karl's eyes widened. "Father, you mean we're going to live with an Aryan family?"

Mr. Rosenthal chuckled dryly. "Not just Aryans, *Christians!* Nathan said they would help us if persecution began here in Poland. Their name is Bedke. I have their address, and the wall won't be completed for several days. Tonight we'll decide what to take with us, then tomorrow I'll go to work as usual." His sigh filled the room. "Tomorrow night, as soon as it's dark, we'll leave."

"What if they won't help us?" Karl whispered. "And if they left Germany because they were under suspicion, won't the Germans be watching them here too?"

Karl saw that his mother looked dazed about this news and that she was fighting back tears. "It's hard to believe this is happening," she moaned.

"Nathan is sure they will help us," Karl's father replied. "We have to take that chance."

Karl's dark eyes were brooding. Nervously he shoved back a stray lock of hair. "What do you want me to do?"

"Get all the food together that we can carry. We don't want to be a burden to the Bedkes." Mr. Rosenthal's brow furrowed deeply. "We'll wear all the clothes we can get on and take only what we absolutely have to have to get by."

"Is it far to where they live?" Sonia asked plaintively.

Moishe nodded. "Far enough." We'll leave right after curfew." He looked away. "It's going to be dangerous, but no more dangerous than if we stay here."

Things were buzzing the next morning. While Mr. Rosenthal went off to work on the gray cinder block wall, the rest of the family began packing what they planned to take with them.

Sonia swept her blond braids back over her shoulders with an angry gesture. "I hate this!" she grumbled.

Karl's lips twisted in a wry smile. "Yes, but the looters are going to be happy!"

Sonia made a move to swat him with a towel. "I can't bear the thought of them barging in here to steal all my things!"

"It's not forever," Karl comforted, sorry for his last remark.

"Make your packs light," Mrs. Rosenthal warned. "We have a long walk ahead of us. And, Karl, bring me your cap."

Karl shrugged and obeyed, having no idea what she wanted with his cap.

"Watch closely, Karl." Mrs. Rosenthal carefully ripped the inside seam of the bill and inserted three gold coins. Then, carefully, she sewed it back together.

Karl's tall lanky frame hovered near the chair where his mother was working. "Why, Mother?"

"In case we are ever separated, Karl, you will have enough money to live for a while. God forbid that should happen, but families are being divided every single day now." She gazed up at him wistfully. "And if you are ever caught, keep alert for some way to escape."

"What about you and Father?"

She would not meet his eyes. "We can manage." She handed back his cap. "There now, see that you never lose it."

When Karl gave his sister a questioning glance, she said in a hushed voice, "Mama sewed money into the lining of my coat."

After a hurried supper of potato pancakes and dark bread, they took a few minutes just before curfew to listen to the latest news.

Moishe bowed his head. "France has fallen. Maybe Hitler will conquer the world after all."

"Don't say that!" his wife snapped. "The allies will come and drive them back, you'll see!"

"I hope so, Golda, I hope so. Now, Karl, Sonia, quickly, quickly, we have no time to waste!"

Karl watched his father closely as he heaved the bag of potatoes onto his broad shoulder. He always stood so tall and straight, and it worried Karl that now his father appeared stooped and weary.

Once outside, Mr. Rosenthal turned briefly. "Stay close and don't talk. Thank God there's no moon to give us away."

Shadows were deep and the night was cool. They waited by the new wall several minutes before crossing the street. Because of the blackout there was no light anywhere. They detected no soldiers.

Trudging away from the street they crept down black alleys overflowing with garbage. Karl lifted his head and sniffed. Ah, they were near Mr. Wrona's bakery. The fresh smell of baking bread sent his senses reeling. But . . . why was Mr. Wrona baking this time of night?

The smell grew stronger. Just when they were at the back of the bakery, the door suddenly creaked open and a dark shadow stood beside them.

Mr. Wrona! Karl whispered the name to himself. The baker! Mr. Wrona was Polish and had always been kind to them. But things were different now. Poles were turning in Jews every day. Would he begin yelling, "Jews! Jews! Police, I have some Jews here!"

"Who's there?" the baker hissed.

Karl could hear his father breathing. "Please, Mr. Wrona, I'm only trying to get my family to safety."

Because Mr. Wrona had opened the door to get rid of some garbage, he had turned off the lights inside the bakery. "Moishe?" His voice was full of disbelief. "If you're caught out after curfew they'll shoot you!"

"I know that, but, Mr. Wrona, they're closing us into a ghetto. We have a place to go if only we can get there."

The door opened wide. "Inside quickly! Hurry!"

The Rosenthals did not hesitate but stepped into the darkened bakery. They waited together while Mr. Wrona turned on a light.

Mr. Wrona was a squat, bald little man with a big heart, and he had nothing against the Jews. "The Germans, those swine!" he snarled. "I spit on them!"

Karl felt pretty sure he would have spit if he had not been inside the bakery. It was a custom in Poland to spit at something they detested.

"Do you have food?" the baker asked quickly.

Moishe sighed. "A bag of potatoes is about all we have left."

"Listen," Mr. Wrona confided, his voice low, "tonight I have been ordered to bake a hundred loaves of bread for the Germans." He winked slyly. "But who is going to count, right?" And he shoved two loaves of dark rye bread into Karl's trembling hands. "Now. Wait until I turn the lights back off and you can slip away."

Moishe wrung the man's hand. "Thanks, Mr. Wrona, you're a good friend."

"Ach! What are friends for?" He opened the door. "Be careful and may Jesus Christ protect you."

Karl hid the warm bread inside his shirt, then buttoned his coat over it. It felt good. But he was puzzled and longed to ask his father why Mr. Wrona had asked Jesus Christ to protect them. Of course, Poland was a Catholic country so maybe he said that to everyone. Since the Jews did not speak the name of Jesus, though, it seemed strange and Karl pondered it for a long time.

An hour passed. Two hours. They threaded their way through alley after alley and darted across dark streets like ghosts. Danger lurked in the shadows. When they caught sight of German soldiers they pressed into the shadows praying that the Eternal would protect them. Once Karl was sure they had been seen, and for the next ten minutes imagined the thud of bullets striking his back. It was so real it was all he could do to keep from running in panic.

Once they all stopped and peeled off their armbands that declared their identity. But what good did that do? If they were seen after curfew they would be shot anyway. And their papers were a dead giveaway. Besides, all but Sonia looked so very Jewish. Karl sighed. He figured that three dark-eyed Jews were about as hard to hide as a elephant in a chicken yard! When they reached the Bedke home it was twelve-thirty. Like every home in Warsaw, it was totally dark because of the blackout curtains. Within, all was still.

Weary and breathless because of all the running and the tension, Moishe Rosenthal drew in a deep breath, lifted his hand and knocked on the door.

Karl's heart thumped. His stomach was in a knot. He was trembling. His legs were weak. "Please, God," he prayed, "don't let them turn us away!"

Danger in the Shadows

The Jews had all made it out of the dining room in record time and were back in the secret rooms. Franz heard his father's harsh breathing, saw him twist his neck, bracing himself, trying to calm his spirit.

Franz and his mother hurriedly scanned the room to make certain everything was back to normal. Extra chairs were scooted under the table. The remains of the coffee was poured out and the pot stowed away. By the time Mr. Bedke reached the door, only three places were set at the table. Breathlessly Franz and Ruth Bedke sat down and picked up apricot dumplings.

"Lord Jesus, help us," Mr. Bedke whispered, as he turned off the lights and opened the door.

"Herr Bedke?" a voice asked urgently.

"Yes?"

"Please, Herr Bedke, we are Jews!"

Mr. Bedke did not hesitate, but flung open the door. "Inside! Quickly!"

Seconds late the Rosenthals stood in the living room and the lights were turned back on.

"Did anyone see you?"

It wasn't, "What is your name?" or "How did you know to come here?" Not anymore. It was only, "Were you seen?"

"No. No one saw us," Moishe Rosenthal assured him. "We were very careful." He was gasping for breath. "A ghetto, Herr Bedke, they are closing us in. We pray God you don't turn us away!"

"We would never turn you away."

Franz heard the words with a sinking heart. Wasn't there *anyone* else in all of Warsaw who would have taken them in?

"Put down your things and come meet my family," Mr. Bedke went on. "Are you hungry? My wife made apricot dumplings."

The Jewish family felt heavy and fat in their many layers of clothing, but they put down their things and followed Hermann Bedke to the dining room.

"This is my wife Ruth and my son Franz. Sit down, tell us who you are, and my wife will make us some tea."

By now Franz knew many of the tricks in stretching the food. One was to put crushed rose leaves in the tea to make it last.

Mr. Rosenthal sat down at the table. He appeared too overcome with the kindness of these Gentiles to speak. When he could, he said, "I'm Moishe Rosenthal. This is my wife Golda and my children, Sonia and Karl. I'm so sorry, all we could bring you was the rest of our potatoes. Things are very bad where we were."

Hermann Bedke waved a hand. "We are getting low on food, but I have a bakery, and as long as we have bread we will survive."

Both Karl and Franz were standing, one on each side of the table. Quietly they measured each other, though they tried to hide that fact. Franz knew there were times when he wore his fourteen years badly, and this was one of those times. He felt awkward and self-conscious and wondered if his lack of confidence showed through. Gazing at the dark, handsome Jewish youth, Franz could only find comfort in the fact that Karl, too, seemed nervous and ill at ease.

"My cousin—" Moishe started to explain.

Mr. Bedke laughed heartily, and Franz didn't see one thing funny. "I know, I know! All our people have a cousin, a friend, or a brother who hid in our home in Germany."

Karl looked as shocked as his parents. "You have others?"

Mr. Bedke nodded. "Oh yes! Ten of them. Fourteen now. I guess God knows how many to send, and if He can use us to save your lives it will be worth the risk."

"You're a good man." Moishe shook his head wordlessly, unable to say more.

To avoid Karl's scrutiny, Franz picked up the apricot dumplings and passed them around. "They're really good. Mother made them this afternoon." When the Jews hesitated, Franz had a quick flash of understanding. Jews did not eat pork. "It's all right. They're made with butter, not lard."

At this, the Rosenthals accepted the dumplings eagerly and began to eat. Karl settled down at the table and Franz sat down across from him.

"You must have secret rooms," Karl observed after a time.

"Two," Franz supplied. "One upstairs and one downstairs." They spent forty-five minutes getting acquainted, but it was late and they were all tired.

"I suggest we turn in." Mr. Bedke rose from the table. "I'm glad you brought blankets because we've used the last of ours. Now let's see . . . I think Sonia should sleep upstairs. There's barely enough room to squeeze in one more. Mr. and Mrs. Rosenthal, you'll have to sleep in the basement. It's damp and musty, but we feel it may be too dangerous for everyone to sleep here in the main house."

Ruth Bedke tried not to yawn. "In the morning we'll fill you in on what's expected of you and the secrecy that has to be observed."

Franz bit his lip, wondering where Karl was going to sleep.

"Oh, and Karl," Franz's father said suddenly, "there is a spare bed in Franz's room, so you'll sleep there. Besides, the secret room is just across his wall if you need to hide in a hurry."

Franz flinched. *There goes the rest of my privacy,* he thought with a sigh.

The Rosenthals were given brief introductions to their roommates and Franz took Karl up to his room.

"Do you have pajamas?" Franz made himself ask.

Karl smiled ruefully. "Yes, somewhere under all these clothes!" Three layers later he found his pajamas. "I never had a Goy for a friend," he said timidly.

Franz hoped his voice sounded deep and didn't crack. "There sure are a lot of names for non-Jews. Goyim, Aryan, Gentile. . . ."

"Don't feel bad," Karl said with a twisted smile, "there are plenty of names for Jews too."

Franz sobered. "I know." He turned out the light and went to stand at the window. Now he could part the blackout curtains and peer outside to the darkened street below.

Wait a minute! What was that anyhow? Some sort of movement or . . . a shadow?

"Karl? Come take a look."

"What's wrong?" Karl crept to his side. "What do you see?"

Franz pointed. "Look over there. No, this way. Do you see something or is it my imagination?"

Karl squinted, trying to see. "I'm not sure."

Franz grew rigid. His blue eyes strained. Oh no! What he saw was real, all right! There was a furtive movement in the shadows!

"Karl, someone down there is watching our house!"

Arrested!

"How can that be?" Karl whispered. He sounded limp and defeated. Terrified. "We were so careful."

Franz, too, was badly frightened. Cold prickles of fear raced along his spine and he felt like someone had punched him in the stomach. "The Germans are everywhere," he muttered. "Someone may have spotted you without you knowing."

As they continued to watch, the figure below slunk into some shrubs. There, he lit a cigarette and quickly cupped his hands around it, but the glowing tip marked his presence clearly.

"I've got to tell my dad about this," Franz said softly. The trouble was, no one could do anything about it. If anyone tried to leave the house he'd be a walking target. No one could possibly get away now.

Karl shivered. "We were so careful, Franz, we never meant to put you in danger!"

Franz nodded grimly and tried not to sound bitter. "Hiding Jews is a terrible crime." He moved away. "I've got to tell Dad."

"Wait," Karl said, putting out a hand.

"What?"

"He's leaving. He just ground out his cigarette and headed down the street."

"He could be going after the SS. I'm still going to wake Dad."

Though there was no need to tiptoe, Franz found himself doing just that. For all he knew, other soldiers could even now be surrounding the house. Any moment the doors could crash open and

47

the feared SS in their black uniforms and boots could come charging inside, searching for Jews. The thought made him shudder.

He tapped on the door to his parents' room. When there was no answer, he rapped louder. "Pssst! Mom! Dad! Wake up!"

A sleepy grunt was his reply. Someone was turning over in bed.

"*Dad!* Dad, wake up! Our house was being watched!"

This statement brought immediate results. Franz could hear his father tumbling out of bed in a hurry. Next instant he was swinging open the door. "Franz, what did you say?"

"We saw someone watching the house, me and Karl," Franz explained quickly. "He just stood there in the shrubbery for a long time and then walked away. Dad, someone must have followed the Rosenthals after all!"

Even though Franz could not actually see his father in the darkness, he could feel his tension. "Where's Karl now?"

"In my room."

"Franz, get him into the secret room. Right now. I know it's crowded, but we can't take chances. Then I want you to smooth up the bed he would have been sleeping in. After that, you go to bed as though nothing has happened. Do you understand?"

Franz nodded his blond head. "I know what to do." He'd been through things like this before and knew exactly what needed to be done. He could even feel the old chill of fear creeping over him, paralyzing him.

The bedroom door closed softly and he could hear his father telling his mother what was going on. There was tight control in his dad's voice and terrible alarm in his mother's. Franz had bad, bad feelings about this dark and ominous night.

Franz raced back to his own room and tugged at Karl's pajama sleeve. "You have to get in the secret room. If that soldier decided that nothing was wrong, then you can sleep in here tomorrow night."

In the faint light filtering in through the blackout curtains which Franz had pulled aside, Karl nodded. He felt deep gratitude to these strange Goyim who were willing to help his people. These strange *Christian* Goyim.

Now there was a puzzle. Didn't the Germans who persecuted the Jews have on their belt buckles the words, *Gott mit uns?* And didn't that mean, *God with us?* So if they claimed to be Christians, then why were the Bedkes so different? Sometime Karl would have to try and sort all that out.

"Here, Karl," Franz was saying in a hushed voice, "through the bookcase!"

Lifting out the bottom shelf he prodded Karl through the secret panel.

"Tell the others what's going on so they'll be especially quiet."

"Can we come out again in the morning?" Karl's voice was anxious and worried.

"Sure. We'll tell you when."

As soon as Karl was through the opening, Franz replaced the panel and then the bookshelf. But when he laid back on his bed he was still fighting the panic. Wide awake, he stared at the blackened ceiling. His heart was uttering frantic, half-formed prayers. It was a night of terror and danger and waiting. Waiting. . . .

The doors crashed open at two-fifteen that morning. Powerful torches flashed light around the house. Boots thudded across the floor and up the stairs.

Franz cringed beneath the sheet. His body, went rigid. Here it was, the thing he had lived through in his mind a thousand times. Both in Germany and in Poland. Now it was real and horrifying and nothing on earth could stop it.

Gathering the last shreds of his courage, Franz crept to the door of his room and opened it just enough to peer out. His father's face was clearly outlined in the brilliant glow of one of the torches. Behind the light SS officers in black uniforms and boots stood stiff and full of rage. Their red armbands were dull in the half light, but the black swastikas inside those white circles stood out like headlights, announcing terror and doom.

Hermann Bedke's face was stoic and calm. Never once did he blink in the harsh light. Hair tousled from sleep he asked in a steady voice, "What is it you want?"

"Don't play games!" one of the officers snapped. "Tell us where you're hiding the dirty, stinking Jews!"

"Dirty, stinking Jews?" Mr. Bedke repeated, looking puzzled. "I have never in my life known a Jew that fit such a description."

Franz told himself that he was almost a man now. He must be courageous. But when his door was suddenly wrenched open and he was flung back against the wall, his bravado crumbled. Dazed and helpless, he watched as one of the officers began pounding the walls with the butt of his rifle, trying to find the secret room.

A movement as his side caused him to whirl. It was his father, pale and trembling now that he knew the hideout would be discovered. To late he realized that he should have reinforced the wall with bricks so it wouldn't sound hollow.

"God help us all!" he whispered fervently.

One of the officers struck the thin wall and grinned with delight. Quickly he smashed the wall and shone his light through the opening.

"*Out!*" he thundered. "All of you, out!"

Franz closed his eyes. All his life he had been told to call upon the name of Jesus when in trouble or danger. Now, with sinking heart, he could only mouth the words, "Jesus, Jesus, Jesus."

One by one the Jews stepped through the crude opening and into the light. Without mercy, the officers pushed and shoved them out of the bedroom and down the stairs.

Like Franz, Karl stood tall and straight, desperately trying to prove his soon-coming manhood.

"You, Jew-lover!" one of the men said fiercely, looking at Franz. "Since you love them so much, get over there with them!" The man's eyes looked like a cold winter night, and Franz obeyed woodenly.

Franz's parents waited helplessly to one side. Ruth Bedke fought desperately to keep from running to her son's side, but such an action could prove fatal for them all.

When an officer came up the basement stairs and reported that there was no secret room there, they all felt relief and thankfulness, but no one dared show these feelings. Maybe, just maybe, some of them could be saved on this awful, awful night.

THE PRISON TRAIN

The SS watched with glee as Franz's mother sobbed, wanting to help him. He heard his father cry out, "Leave my son out of this! He had nothing to do with it!"

No one answered. It was as if they had not heard. *They don't care,* Franz told himself mournfully. *How crazy can things get? The Jews are guilty just because they're Jews and we're guilty because we tried to help them.*

Karl's sister Sonia had been shoved inside a lorry that had already moved off down the darkened street. Strangely, all the Jews from the secret room were with her except for Karl.

The boys were allowed only to get dressed, put on their coats and take along Franz's rucksack. At the last minute Karl grabbed a blanket. After that they were shoved inside another lorry that rumbled away into the night.

They traveled without headlights. It came as a shock to both Franz and Karl that the lorry had many other Jewish boys in it. Some of the smaller ones were crying. Franz was the only Gentile present. Under the thick canvas a deep sense of gloom covered them all. A soldier sat near the opening with a rifle across his knees to make sure no one escaped.

"They'll kill us," Karl stated firmly. "I heard that they take away the Jewish kids and shoot them."

Franz was bumping up and down in the rugged vehicle. "They won't shoot us, Karl. Somehow we have to escape."

51

They huddled together in despair, Jew and Gentile. Jammed together so tightly, Franz could feel Karl's breath on his neck when he spoke.

"How *can* we escape?" Karl whispered.

"I don't know yet."

"There's no way for us to get off this lorry," Karl worried.

"Not now. Later."

"Do you have a plan?"

"No. Karl, we have to pray and ask God to show us."

Karl knew that people like the Bedkes prayed, but didn't they talk to Jesus Christ? Wasn't that why they were called *Christians?* Yet Franz sounded as if he was talking about the God Karl knew. It got more and more confusing as he thought about it. Maybe one day he would ask Franz to explain.

"I can't believe my mother and dad have been arrested," Franz agonized.

"I'm sorry, Franz. It makes me feel so guilty, You were willing to hide us, and my parents are still safe, while yours. . . ." He sighed and did not finish.

Franz buried his face in his hands. He could still hear his mother begging for his life. Still hear the last words his father had spoken to him.

"Mein liebes Sohn, bleib gesund, halt Mut!"

The words meant, "My dear son, keep well, be courageous!"

Franz's eyes grew moist. For a long, terrifying moment he wanted to be a child again so he could cry like the younger boys were doing. His hand went to the hem of his coat, where his mother had sewn in the marks and zlotys. Right now that money meant nothing. He would gladly have thrown it away just to be back home where it was warm and safe. Instead, he was accused of one of the greatest crimes in the Third Reich, that of hiding Jews.

Someone in the lorry yelped when another boy accidentally kicked him. An older boy was sniffing and trying not to break down. At the opening into the lorry the soldier hurled constant racial slurs and insults at them.

For hours they roved through the night, leaving the city behind. No one except the officers knew where they were bound.

"Do you have any idea where they're taking us?" Karl asked once, his voice low and quivery.

"No."

"Franz, I'm so sorry for getting you into this."

Franz shrugged. "You don't have to keep apologizing. Anyway, maybe it wasn't even your fault. For all we know they may have been watching our house since the very first Jews came."

"I want to go home!" a child wailed miserably. His answer was a vicious kick from the German soldier. The boy screamed and sat sniffling and silent.

Franz put his hand on the boy's shoulder. "Don't panic," he said quietly. "We all have to be brave right now."

The boy gazed toward Franz in the bumping darkness but still kept sniffling.

They were deep in rolling hills when the lorry eventually pulled through a barbed wire enclosure. A gate was immediately pulled shut behind them. Everything was in darkness. The boys could hear harsh voices, then the soldier leaped to the ground and began hauling them out of the lorry.

Brutal hands shoved them forward. The dark blur of some huge detainment center lay before them. There they were forced to stand at attention for four hours. No reason was given: it was an order.

Franz made sure his rucksack was in his possession and Karl kept the warm blanket folded under one arm.

Karl glanced at Franz. "This is no way to make friends," he said wryly.

"Quiet!" a voice bellowed. "No talking!"

"But I'm tired and hungry," a younger boy complained. As a soldier dove at the offender in fury, Karl gripped Franz's wrist, warning him to be quiet.

Tired, hungry, and confused, they were treated like hated animals. Franz glanced at Karl sideways. What a handsome individual he was! Karl was a person, only another person, so how could so many people hate the Jews like this?

He stood with his head high, thinking about that. And this hated war, where Hitler was determined to exterminate all the Jews, forcing them to run and hide and live in terror for their lives.

Is this what they go through all the time? he asked himself. *Always knowing they can be the next to die? Just for being a Jew? It's insane!*

It was one thing to watch the persecution from the warmth and safety of one's home, but now he, Franz, was one of them! Despised, hunted down like a dog—worse!—and shot because....

Suddenly all the bitterness and resentment Franz had battled from the past melted like ice in sunlight. He began to understand how his parents could love these people of God enough to risk everything to save them. And didn't the Bible say something about blessing those who bless the people of Israel?

Karl glanced at him and Franz smiled and nodded. *We're going to make it,* his eyes said.

The next hours were a blur. One person after another asked them questions. The same questions, over and over. Franz's blond good looks irritated the Germans, it seemed, more than anything else, especially when they discovered that he was a German citizen.

"You're a fool!" someone hissed at him. "You could have been a member of Hitler's Youth! You could even have fathered children for the Fuhrer's pure race! Instead you are a Jew-lover!"

Franz looked back into the ice blue eyes and longed to blurt out that the very Man they sang about at Christmas was a Jew.

"Fine!" the voice went on. "Then you can take your place with the Jews. We'll see how you like it then!"

At long last the boys were given a slice of black bread and a bowl of watery potato soup. Later still they fell onto hard bunks covered with a little straw. Each bunk held four or five boys. They were crowded together so tightly that if one turned over they had to all turn.

Neither Karl nor Franz had met anyone else they knew, so they made it a point to stay together. Even though they were strangers, a bond had begun to form between them.

Having had no sleep for more than 24 hours, they fell into deep sleep immediately. But it was only three and a half hours later when a sound broke through their numbed senses. "Gather your belongings! Get ready to move out!"

"Cut that out!" Karl yelled, when the other boys scrambled over top of him.

"Take it easy," Franz encouraged. "We've got to keep our heads."

Karl mumbled something and let his long, lean body drop to the floor. Before going outside, he scooped up the valuable blanket and handed Franz the rucksack.

"That straw made me itch all over!" one boy grumbled.

Another answered, "Why wouldn't it? It was probably full of lice."

Great, Franz thought. The very thought made him want to scratch.

"They're going to shoot us," another boy wailed in dread. "That's what they do to Jews. Or worse."

"I don't think they're going to shoot us," Karl consoled. "At least, not yet. They said for us to gather our belongings, so I think they're just going to take us off somewhere else."

It was still dark outside. Several green army lorries were waiting over by the barbed wire.

"We sure can't escape from the lorry," Karl murmured. "Not with a soldier riding back there with us."

"Karl? Do you pray?"

"Are you crazy?" Karl cried indignantly. "Of course I pray!"

Franz ignored the scorn in Karl's voice. After all, he was pretty sure there were Jews who did *not* pray. "I didn't mean it like that." Outside the building, he fell into line with the others. "I only meant that we'll have to ask God when to escape."

There was a movement around them. Karl and Franz had been so involved whispering to each other that they had not heard the order. Now they came to attention as the endless counting began once more. It seemed to the boys that the Germans did nothing but count their prisoners. Were they so afraid that one of them might disappear?

Daylight crawled into the sky and still the boys had to stand at attention. When it seemed that they would be kept standing all day, there was suddenly another order. Now the boys were marched to the lorries and crammed inside.

Two soldiers sat stoic and silent at the open end of the vehicle as it started away.

"Where are they taking us?" someone whimpered.

"*Silence!*" a voice roared.

Franz was keeping his antenna up. Last night, on the way to the detainment center, Franz thought he had heard the word *Dachau*. The very word send chills through his veins. If they were being taken to Dachau, it was the worst possible news, for they would surely be put to death there. Franz had heard that other terrible things happened to Jews in that concentration camp too.

The lorries did not travel far this time but screeched to a stop near a small train depot. Waiting on the tracks, steaming and hissing, a train was sitting. Franz saw at once that it was not a passenger train, but that a line of cattle cars waited behind the engine.

This is it, Franz told himself forlornly. *They're going to stuff us into those cars and take us away!*

Escape to Nowhere

While the long train chugged and hissed, the boys were once more made to form lines. A voice over loudspeakers blared out constant commands. Soldiers were everywhere. Terror-stricken, the younger boys began to cry.

A soldier walked up and handed the officer in charge a paper and they both nodded. Karl watched as a sly smile wrapped itself around the officer's lips. Then he heard the words, "Good. Dachau was too good for them anyway."

Karl nudged Franz with an elbow and Franz nodded that he had heard. But exactly what did it mean? Something even worse than the concentration camp? Franz felt the blood drain from his head, felt his legs grow weak. Karl's olive-skinned face was pale also and he kept a tight grip on Franz's arm.

After an hour and a half the boys were counted again, then shoved into cattle cars. Since Karl and Franz were two of the first to enter, they pressed to the rear of the car. There they found a pile of black bread, so they knew it was going to be a long trip. A hundred boys were crowded into the cattle car where Franz and Karl stood shivering and terrified. No one could have sat or fallen down if he had wanted to. Two high, small windows gave the only air.

"Help me, Jesus," Franz cried silently, "I'm so scared!"

Oh sure, he was fourteen years old and almost a man, but right now he was just a scared kid who desperately wanted to go home to his parents.

For two hours the train did not move, but sat there hissing and steaming. Young boys were screaming and crying. With so many crammed into the car, the heat was impossible.

"I want to go home!" someone yelped.

"I'm hungry!"

Gathering what he could of his shredded courage, Karl shouted, "Listen! There's bread here. Would you like some bread?"

This news brought those in the front of the car trying to claw their way to the bread.

"Wait!" Franz yelled. "We'll toss it to you, all right?"

A few minutes of calm descended. Karl and Franz busied themselves with getting food to the starving youths. As soon as most of them were happily gnawing the bread, Franz picked up a loaf and thrust it inside his shirt.

"For later," he whispered to Karl. "If we're able to get away, we'll need food."

Karl smiled grimly. "Great idea, Franz. But it doesn't much look like we'll ever be able to escape." He looked up at the high, small windows.

"If we don't try, Karl, they're going to kill us." Franz was quiet for a minute. He was still horrified at what was happening and his heart was lurching as the train was lurching. "If the train stops in a city it'll be plenty rough; but if we stop in the country. . . . " He sighed and his whole body shuddered. "Maybe. Karl," he added desperately, "we have to try!"

The hunger that had been present now turned to thirst. Anger and grumbling broke out. Crowded against each other as they were, sharp elbows began gouging those next to them. Screams and cries of fear and confusion filled the cattle car. Three boys fainted from the heat, but no one could help them.

Long hours passed. Sometimes the train sat on a siding for an hour or more, going nowhere. Then it would jerk forward and rumble down the tracks for a while. Night fell and the heat let up a little. Still the train lumbered along.

"I'm thirsty!" someone wailed.

"Shut up!" howled another. "We're all thirsty!"

"But I have to go to the bathroom!" whimpered yet another.

"So do I!"

It was bedlam inside the cattle car. Franz thought of the thousands of Jews who had endured this senseless cruelty. And waiting at the end of the rides were Hitler's furnaces or some other means of extermination. He shuddered, while shame charged through him once more. How could he have ever been resentful of helping God's chosen people. *How could he?* He bowed his head and felt like crying.

Since there was no water and no bathroom, the smell inside the reeling car soon became unbearable. No one had been to a toilet since yesterday morning and they were all miserable. The younger boys could not take it any longer.

It was senseless, all of it. Waiting on sidings for long hours. Listening to the nearby blast of exploding bombs. Wondering if their train would suddenly go up in splinters of steel and kindling.

"I think we may be heading into Germany," Franz said once. "Do you speak German?"

Karl shrugged. "A little. It's a lot like Yiddish."

Hours dragged like days, and days melted into nights. How many? They had all lost count. Oddly, it didn't seem to matter much anyhow.

They slept on their feet. A feeling of doom settled over them all. Except for outbursts of fighting and arguing, most of the boys now seemed resigned to whatever was about to happen to them.

"If they take us to a concentration camp," Karl murmured, "do you know what they'll do to us?" His dark eyes were full of fear and question marks.

Franz kept his voice low so the other boys could not hear. "I've heard that they dip you in some sort of solution to kill lice, then make you wear striped overalls." He swallowed hard, remembering all the rumors he'd heard. "They—uh—they even shave your heads." Sighing, he passed a hand over his own thick blond hair, still tousled from his last sleep. He had a comb in his rucksack, but everyone was packed too tightly for him to open it. Anyway, with things so horrifying, why should he worry about his hair?

"I hate the Germans!" Karl said fiercely.

Without thinking, Franz replied, "Jesus died for the Germans too, Karl."

Karl stared at him. "What does *He* have to do with anything?"

Franz longed to explain it right then, but he knew he could be asking for a lot of trouble. Everyone was restless and full of hate. Hating Jesus as they did, they could turn on him like a pack of wolves.

"I'll tell you about it later," he promised.

Pale streaks of light filtered into the cattle car. When the train came to a bone-jarring halt, they all hoped it was the end of the line. No matter what was in store for them now, it couldn't be any worse than this nightmarish ride had been.

The bolts in the cattle cars were suddenly drawn and the heavy doors were swung open. The light blinded them for a moment, for they had not seen sunlight in days.

All up and down the tracks boys began spilling out of the cars, wandering around aimlessly. Guards were everywhere, jabbing with their rifle butts, forcing them into a line.

"We're in the country!" Franz whispered. "Look."

Karl peered out the crack in the wall of the car. "What do you think?"

"There are trees just a few yards away. Lots of trees." He darted to the other side, searched for a hole, a crack, anything to see through. "Over here, too, Karl. Have you got bread and the blanket?"

"Yeah." He touched the brim of his cap to assure himself that he also had the money his mother had concealed.

"Listen, Karl, there are hundreds of people out there. When you jump to the ground, look to see if the guards are watching. If they're not, crawl under the train and leap down the ravine on the other side!"

Karl's heart was thundering inside his chest. "They have dogs," he reminded Franz.

"They won't bother us if the guards don't see us escape."

So they had been right: new orders had changed their course from Dachau to . . . *here!* Not that it made a lot of difference. Either place meant death.

Karl gritted his teeth. "I'm ready."

Nearly all the Jewish boys were now off the train. Karl and Franz hung back, following the last few boys from the cattle car. Karl watched in horror as the boys were being pushed and prodded into the woods. For the moment the attention of the guards was upon them.

"Now!" he hissed.

The two boys dropped to the ground amidst the crush of many others, went into a crouch and threw themselves beneath the train. Scrambling over the rails they lunged out the other side and dove down the steep ravine. When they reached the bottom they lay for a long moment, breathless and terrified.

"Did anyone see us?" Franz whispered.

"I don't think so. And they didn't count anyone again. I guess they just wanted to make sure we were all there when we left Warsaw."

The trees began only six yards away, but the boys lay with trembling limbs and pounding hearts for another ten minutes before crawling away.

Too weak to stand, they edged forward on their stomachs. The bread felt warm and soft against their flesh. Dead leaves rustled and crackled under them, sounding like the crack of bullets in their terrified ears. Surely the guards could hear it! Pine needles stuck in their clothing and hair. They expected any minute to hear the shouts of angry guards. The vicious snarl of the dogs. The crack of rifles. The splat of bullets finding their targets.

Neither of them looked back until they were under the cover of trees. Their arms were shaking so badly, both from fear and the effort of pulling their bodies forward, that they collapsed where they were on the ground.

"I can't move," Franz moaned.

Karl lay with his head on his arm. "I still don't believe we did it."

Franz twisted his head to look back. "Maybe we did. There's no one back there. Nobody's yelling. Karl, we've got to get as far away as we can."

At last, two tall youths, one fair and blond, one dark and Jewish, limped to their feet, hung onto trees for a moment, and started away with a lumbering gait into the woods.

Three hundred yards farther on, sweat running down their faces and into their eyes, they stopped to get their breath. The train was now invisible. No human voices could be heard. Only the erratic puffing of steam from the engine of the train broke the deep stillness.

Karl was bent, holding his knees. "I guess der Fuhrer would just about stand on his ear if he knew that two of his *gefangenes* had escaped!"

In their weakness and weariness they giggled like school girls. "You want to know something else?" Karl said when he could talk. "Here I am, running for my life with a Goy and I can't even remember your last name!"

This sent them into more unreasonable peals of laughter. All the horror and tension of the past two days had caught up with them at last. Franz wondered idly if they were having nervous breakdowns.

"Bedke," he said, still giggling. "My last name is Bedke."

Their sense of victory and euphoria was suddenly cut short when the chatter of machine guns fractured the silence. It seemed to go on forever as hundreds of young Jewish boys were mowed down like grass.

Shadows in the Night

Franz dropped his rucksack without a word. A dumb look washed over his face. Blank. He leaned back against the nearest tree, and a moment later slid to the ground like a rag doll.

Karl turned his back, stood tall and stiff. Then he bent double and threw up.

Above, on the slope, the business was finished. Soldiers returned to the train joking and laughing as if they were just coming back from a party. They boarded the train and after a few minutes it chugged away down the tracks.

Karl sat down heavily near Franz. "There's no cause for the world to hate us just because we're Jews!" he shouted angrily.

Franz looked over at him slowly, still stunned at what had happened. "There was another Jew the world hated without a cause, too, Karl," he said sadly.

Karl asked idly, "Who, Franz?"

"Jesus Christ, God's Son."

May Jesus Christ protect you.

It seemed like years had passed since the baker, Mr. Wrona, had spoken those words to the Rosenthals. Karl hadn't understood then and he didn't understand now.

"If only we could have saved them," Karl moaned, anxious to change the subject.

Franz pulled up his knees and laid his head on them. "I wish we could have." The steady rat-a-tat-tat of the machine gun still echoed through his head. "Karl, that's why we had to run from Germany to

Poland. If we had stayed, a lot of people would have died. The way it was, we were able to save some."

He knew it was true. If they had tried to drag some of the boys along with them, they would have been detected and they would all have been shot down like dogs.

"Karl? Is this the way it is for the Jews all the time?"

"All the time, ever since Hitler came to power. If people don't take them in, they're done for." And he thought of his old friend Jankele.

"We have to have some kind of a plan, Karl. Think of some way to make it now that we've managed to escape." He sighed.

"We have to go . . . somewhere."

"Are you scared, Franz?"

Franz was still sitting against the tree. He nodded. "Sure." He wanted to add, "I'm fourteen and I'm trying hard to be brave, prove my manhood! But it's really tough being a kid and a man at the same time!"

"It's getting dark, Franz. We have to find a place to spend the night." He looked around. "It's too bad we don't have a map or compass."

Franz showed a little interest. "Wait, Karl, let's see what's in here." He opened the rucksack and began to paw through the contents. "Well," he said wryly, "I guess you can tell it was my mother who packed this. She put in a needle and thread, but no compass or map."

They tromped forward through the woods, still trying to put the other boys out of their minds. Brooding did no good. They couldn't help them.

"It's warm anyway," Karl reminded his companion. He snagged his shirt on a low branch and stopped to free it. "If we find a haystack, we could sleep there."

The sun was half over the horizon. A cool breeze started up. Shadows danced among the trees. They came to a cold stream and drank, then ate some of their bread.

"I wonder what they did with Sonia," Karl said balefully, more to himself than to Franz.

"Try not to worry, Karl. She's so blond, maybe they think she's adopted. You know, a Pole."

"Not all Poles and Germans are blond, Franz," Karl reminded him.

Franz sighed. "Karl, I know how you feel. My parents were arrested too, remember? And I think about that. But, look, we could go on and on, worrying about whether they've found *your* mother and dad. But worrying won't help anyone. It's like those—those boys . . . there's nothing we can do."

Karl kicked his way through some thick pine needles. "I know you're right, Franz. It's still hard to deal with."

The moon slid into the sky, a milky-looking half moon that did little to penetrate the woods and help the boys see where they were going. They walked in dismal silence, shadows of the night, going nowhere.

"If only my mother had thought to put a torch in my rucksack!" Franz moaned. "I guess she didn't really think I'd ever have to use any of the stuff she put in." He tried to put some hope into his next words. "Anyway, we may come to a farm where the people will want to help us."

"Are you kidding?" Karl scoffed. "The Poles aren't wild about us Jews!"

"But, Karl, I'm positive we're in Germany, and a lot of the Germans are willing to help."

"I don't know, Franz. Even a German farmer could blow the whistle on us."

The night of shadows became eerie and frightening. Sometimes now they broke into the open, where a potato field became a great lake that must be skirted. Trees, with their outstretched limbs, were grotesque monsters. A single tree in a field became a watcher, waiting to view them better so he could sic the SS on them. Any shadow that moved was menacing and terrifying. Then there was a mysterious sound that sent the two youths into a defensive crouch. A shuddering, flapping noise.

Two great white objects, weaving and flapping wildly, lunged at them from out of the darkness.

"Out, Out, On With You!"

As the menacing white shapes lunged at the boys, fluttering and billowing, they felt flat on their faces to the ground. Their hands came up to cover their heads and they lay trembling and terrified.

For long moments neither of them spoke, but continued to cower in dread. Franz tried to pray, but the prayer stuck in his throat.

After what seemed an eternity and the ghostly things did not attack, Karl peeked out with his right eye. Odd . . . the things were still there, white and ominous in the darkness, but they had not come any nearer.

"Franz?" he whispered.

"Yeah?"

"Look."

Franz had absolutely no desire to challenge or investigate the leaping, menacing white objects. But he figured if Karl was brave enough to take a look, then he had better do the same.

He rose slowly to his knees and elbows, ready to make a mad dash for safety if necessary. Peering cautiously through his fingers, he saw that the deadly, lurching monsters appeared even larger and more threatening than before. There were two of them, and they rushed and dove at the terrified youths. Then, strangely, they would recede, seem to gather strength, and lunge forward again. When rushing forward, they billowed, but when they retreated, they went almost flat.

Karl was struggling to hold back another senseless burst of hysterical laughter.

"What?" Franz demanded warily. "What's so funny?"

"We've got to be close to a farm house," Karl said, his voice low and sheepish. "Don't you know what those things are?"

Franz felt a little irritated and wished Karl wouldn't sound so sure of himself. "No. "Do you?"

"Sheets!" the Jewish boy announced in a majestic whisper. "Someone left sheets on the line to dry overnight!"

Franz stared toward Karl for a long time in silence, then looked back at the snapping, ballooning apparitions so close to them in the darkness. "I can't believe it," he admitted ruefully. "We were afraid of *sheets?*"

It was all the tension of the past days and they both knew it. They were all tied up in knots. Their nerves were shot. After all, neither of them had ever been arrested. They had never been in a cattle car, heading for certain death. Nor had either of them ever been lost in the woods. Now, with their imaginations running wild, each new, release was apt to bring on a fit of nervous laughter.

"Well," Karl sputtered, "all I can say is, I'm glad no one was around to see us scared out of our wits by a couple of sheets!"

They stood on shaky feet and stared for a long moment at the ghostly sheets threatening them.

That was the night when a true bond began to form between the two youths.

"I can't see a house," Franz said, "but there has to be one close by."

"I think we're by a garden, Franz. The ground is soft like it's been plowed."

Franz felt along the ground and his groping hand found a small potato. Then another and another. Since they were so small they had evidently been left there.

"Are you hungry?"

"Are you kidding?" Karl replied. "Is Hitler the Fuhrer?"

"I found some potatoes."

"Really?" Karl knelt excitedly and began gathering the little vegetables for himself.

Brushing off the dirt, they ate them with the remainder of their bread.

Stowing some more potatoes into their shirts for later, they crept forward. Dogs began barking, hearing them approach, and the boys fled back into the woods.

The night crawled past. Sometimes, because of the blackness of the night, they stepped into gurgling streams. Other times the ground beneath their feet grew soft and marshy and they sidestepped quickly to avoid it. Deep gullies and high rolling hills continually surprised them and they often fell headlong down slopes and into unexpected brush.

"Winter's going to be on top of us soon," Karl mumbled, sharing his thoughts. He stroked back his snarled black curls. "We can't survive it in the open like this."

Franz ran into a low tree branch and stopped quickly to untangle his thick slab of blond hair. "I know. But, Karl, God has been with us so far. He's not going to let us down."

Karl thought about that. " 'Be strong and of good courage, fear not, nor be afraid of them; for the Lord thy God, he it is who doth go with thee; he will not fail thee, nor forsake thee.' " Karl's voice sounded suddenly strong and fearless. "That's Deuteronomy 31:6."

Franz smiled " 'For he hath said, I will never leave thee nor forsake thee.' Hebrews 13:5."

Karl stared at Franz in stunned amazement. "Your Goyim Bible says that?"

"Karl, it's not a Goyim Bible! It's a Jewish Bible! It was all written by Jews except for the gospel of Luke. Luke was a Greek, but the rest of the New Testament was written by Jews."

Karl frowned darkly. The pieces to this mystery were too great for him to try and put together. Besides, he didn't want to think about it. Things were confusing enough the way it was.

"It's cold," Karl muttered finally. He put on the coat he had been lugging around all this time. "You have matches, Franz; could we have a fire?"

"I don't think that's such a good idea, Karl. We don't have any idea who may be roaming around these woods in the dark, and fires can be seen a long way off."

Farms, it seemed, were few and far between. Occasionally they could hear the barking of dogs. The sound was alarming and stressful.

Then the trees parted abruptly and they became aware of some sort of stubble under their shoes. The moon had become a weak, watery thing that dangled in heavy gray clouds.

Neither boy saw the haystack until they were six feet away from it. In the heavy night moisture they could now smell the newness of it.

"It's dry," Karl announced gravely, "but it won't be for long."

Franz reached out a hand to test it. "Long enough."

As the first great drops of cold rain began striking the ground, they burrowed deeply into the haystack and pulled it back around them. It was scratchy to their exposed flesh, but it was also warm and sweet-smelling; and it had been a very long and terrifying day. They did not speak to each other but nestled into the soft warmth silently. Their eyes slammed shut and they went deep into sleep.

The rain struck their refuge like nails, but it didn't last long and they remained dry.

It was the steamy warmth that wakened them. Yet it took several minutes before they could remember exactly where they were and what had happened to bring them there.

Stomachs rumbling with hunger, they pushed aside the hay and stepped out into bright sunshine. Their clothing was full of hay. It matted their hair and stuck out of their cuffs and collars. Franz had torn open the knee of his trousers somewhere and hay protruded from the hole, along with one knobby knee.

"They could hang us from poles and use us for scarecrows," Karl grumbled.

Franz looked around. Far away in front of him and to his right he saw a farmhouse, where a thin trail of gray smoke rose from a cook stove. A dog barked shrilly.

"Let's duck back into the woods and build a fire so we can roast the potatoes," Franz suggested. "A small fire would be hard to spot in broad daylight."

Karl was still wrestling with the hay caught in his hair. Franz thought he looked discouraged and afraid. Desperate. If they should get caught, after all, Franz had his old German papers and his blond hair and blue eyes. Karl had nothing except his Jewish looks, including a slightly hawkish nose. There was just one thing Karl wasn't counting on: Franz would never leave him. Not now. They had already been through too much together. Besides, it wouldn't take the SS long before they realized Franz's crime against the Third Reich. No, they would stick together, no matter what the future held.

Going back into the woods some fifty yards, they paused to examine their surroundings. The sound of the dogs were faraway now and no threat to them.

"Do you think the Germans come into the woods?" Karl whispered.

Franz scooped back his hair and dropped his lanky body to the ground. "Sure they do. But I doubt if any would be around so early. Come on, Karl, help me gather some dry twigs."

Karl thought for a minute. "I heard somewhere that the low, dry branches of pine trees make a smokeless fire."

Franz glanced up. "Really? Let's try it."

He rummaged around in the rucksack for the matches, and his groping fingers encountered the needle and thread. "Karl? Do you know how to sew?"

"You're kidding, aren't you? I never touched a needle in my life. Why?"

"I just poked a pine cone into my knee because of that hole." He sighed. "I guess I'll have to learn how to sew."

Karl raised his dark eyebrows. "We'll probably both have to learn before this is over."

They roasted their potatoes and thought they had never eaten anything so good. But the fear and uncertainty of their present situation pressed in upon them at once.

"The war could last for a long time, Franz. Maybe years. We have to face it: we cannot survive that long." Karl peered up at the sharp glint of sunlight coming through the trees. "Winter is right around the corner, and you know how cold it gets in this part of the world!"

Franz had laid his coat to one side. Now he dragged it over and ran his thumb and finger along the hem. "I have some money, Karl. Mother sewed some German marks and some Polish zlotys in the hem of my coat. And I look older than fourteen, I know I do! If things get really bad, I can rent us a room somewhere and then get a job in a factory."

"Making bullets and grenades to kill more Jews?" Karl asked bitterly.

"No, Karl! You know I didn't mean that!"

"I have three gold coins that my mother sewed into the brim of my cap," Karl offered lamely. "I don't know how we could ever sell them though."

"We'll find a way. Karl, remember the verses of scripture we talked about before? They're just as true this minute as they were then."

Karl smiled ruefully. "I know they are. It just feels so hopeless."

A twig snapped somewhere and both youths bolted upright to stare through the shadows of the trees. Still tense and anxious, every noise alerted them to possible danger. The sound, though, was not repeated and they began to relax.

"We're going to have to hide in the woods during the day," Franz told his companion, "and walk at night."

"And just where are we walking to?" Karl asked dolefully.

"A farm. We have to find a farm where the people are willing to hide us. Karl," Franz said desperately, "it's the only way!"

Karl gulped in a deep breath of air. "Tell me something. Was it just your parents who loved my people? Or," and the brown eyes probed Franz deeply, "did you love them too?"

The words stung Franz. "It wasn't that I ever disliked the Jews. To me, they were just people like everyone else." He swallowed the swift guilt that seized him. "It was . . . well, I could never bring home friends. I guess you'd say I lived a secret life along with everyone else in the house. So I did get to resenting them being with us."

Karl dropped his gaze. "I figured as much."

"But, Karl, I always knew about their special place in history! I always knew they were God's chosen people. Like I said before, Jews gave us the Bible, the prophets and . . . they gave us the Messiah, Jesus. No," he added slowly, "I never hated the Jews. How could I not love them when my Saviour was a Jew?"

Karl swiftly began scooping handfuls of dirt on the fire. Talking about the Messiah in this way made him irritated, made him want to lash out, argue.

"We can't just sit here all day!" he snapped. "We have to find food, even if we have to steal it."

"We don't have to steal, Karl. I have some dried food that my mother put in the rucksack. If we don't eat it all at once, it should last us two or three days." Franz hesitated. "Karl? I want you to know that I don't have any resentment in my heart for you or your people anymore."

Karl gave him a long look and finished putting out the fire. "You might as well be Jewish yourself now," he said quietly.

Franz nodded. "That's how I've got it figured."

They wandered the rest of the day. Sometimes they thought perhaps they were going around in circles. Especially when the fields and the gullies all seemed identical. But always they stayed within the trees, never venturing out into the open. After all, the German soldiers could be anywhere—and often were.

At sundown they saw a cultivated area, and beyond that a farm house. Smoke poured from the chimney, clothes streamed from the clothesline, and a dog rushed toward them snarling, hackles raised.

"Don't move," Franz instructed. "Don't look it in the eye or it may think you're challenging it." He dropped to one knee and realized too late it was the knee with the hole in the trousers.

A small, sharp pebble bit into his knee with stabbing pain and he recoiled.

The dog was big and shaggy, black with a white chest. His lips were drawn back in a vicious snarl and ominous growls rose from his throat.

"Please, God!"

Franz lurched forward again, fighting to ignore the pain in his knee. Without looking the animal in the eye, he held out a friendly hand, palm downward.

"Good boy. Good dog. Come on, boy. Good dog."

For reply, the dog crouched to spring. The fur along his neck and back was raised sharply.

Karl hung back, staring and praying. He felt pale beneath his olive skin and his arms and legs were covered with goose bumps.

"Easy. Easy, boy. Good dog."

The staring, glassy eyes of the animal gradually softened. Its fur flattened again. The savage white teeth were not quite so alarming, though snuffling growls still fell from the dog's throat.

"Come on, boy. It's all right," Franz crooned softly, encouraging the dog to be friends. He was fully aware that an animal like this could tear them to pieces.

The animal slunk forward. The wet black nose stretched to sniff Franz's hand. As if deciding that the youth was harmless, it fell to its belly and crawled toward him.

Feeling somewhat more courageous, Karl stepped forth, kneeling and holding out his hand. He had never owned a dog and knew little about them, but, together, he and Franz began stroking the rough fur and scratching the animal's ears.

Karl raised a brow. "What now?"

Franz stood slowly, keeping a friendly hand on the dog's neck and speaking gently. "Now we are going to the farm house and ask if we can sleep in the hayloft tonight."

"Do you really think they will let us do that?"

Franz sighed. "I guess there's only one way to find out."

As they neared the house, the rich, fragrant aroma of borscht drifted out to them like fog. Hungry as they were, the effect was dizzying.

"Karl, wait."

"What?"

Franz opened his rucksack and began rummaging around. "We must look like a couple of escaped prisoners!" He listened to his own words. "I guess that's because we are," he added with a shrug. "But let's at least comb our hair."

Without water or oil, Franz's straight hair was still unruly and fell over one eye. Karl's curly black hair was snarled and even harder to work with.

"I hope I look a little better," Franz murmured. "You look great with all that curly hair."

Dirty and disheveled, they walked across the yard. It was littered with broken wagon wheels, boards, a shed where sleeping chickens murmured and gurgled in their dreams, and a great heap of straw. Nervously, Franz reached forth a hand and knocked at the door. A naphtha lamp burned somewhere in the house, sending out a fellow glow where shadows flickered and danced.

The door opened a crack and a plump little woman in a flour smeared apron and drooping gray hair stood before them. She shivered under the shawl that was wrapped around her shoulders and peered at them through dirty wire-framed glasses. "Ja?"

"We, uh. . . ."

Before either of the boys could explain their presence, the woman darted back inside to pick up the lamp. Bringing it to the door, she looked at them intently. "Jews!" she exclaimed. "Don't you know. . . . "

"Please!" Franz cut in desperately. "We just want to sleep in your loft tonight. We're so tired and—"

"And hungry, too, eh?" The door opened a little wider and the woman's face softened somewhat. "I am sorry things must be so bad for the Jews. That Hitler!" She glanced about furtively, hesitated. "How early can you be up and on your way?"

"Early!" Karl promised rashly. "Sunup!"

The woman looked over her shoulder, jerked her head. "My man is sleeping off his whiskey, eh? But you, if you will promise to go early in the morning, you can stay in the loft." Her wrinkled brow knotted with fear. "Me, I defend you, but Hans. . . . Understand?" When the boys nodded, she added quickly, "Off with you then. And wait for me. I bring you some good soup and some bread, ja?" She winked broadly and Franz wanted to hug her.

"So now you are really Jewish," Karl drawled as they headed for the barn.

Franz smiled. "Did you ever doubt it?"

The old woman came ten minutes later, swinging a lantern in one hand and holding a small pail of borscht and bread with the other.

"You're very kind," Karl smiled.

The woman surveyed their dirty faces and tattered clothing, shook her head sadly and left.

Karl offered thanks for the food in Yiddish and the boys gulped it down. Full and thankful, they burrowed into the hay and fell into deep sleep.

It seemed only a moment later when Franz felt something strike his shoe. He turned quickly to avoid whatever it was. When he did a pitchfork stabbed the hay where he had been sleeping.

A startled, bewhiskered old man took a step back, nearly falling from the loft. His eyes were small and beady, and he appeared angry enough to kill them on the spot.

"Jews!" He spat out the word as though it had made his mouth dirty.

Karl was instantly awake and alarmed to see a full shaft of sunlight falling across the loft from an open window. They had overslept after all!

"We're going!" Franz cried quickly. "We didn't bother anything!"

The farmer brandished the pitchfork menacingly as the boys scrambled down the ladder. "Out!" he yelled fiercely. "Out! On with you! Dirty Christ-killers!"

A Hiding Place

With adrenaline pumping through their bodies, Karl and Franz fled for their lives. Their last look back showed them a man brandishing a pitchfork and an anxious woman in a dirty gray dress and shoes without laces with her hand to her mouth.

She was kind to us, Franz prayed frantically, *please don't let her be in trouble with her husband!*

Karl's heart hammered in his ears. He had once more been plunged into a whirlpool of confusion, but he said nothing until they were safely out of sight in the woods again.

Hungry, breathless, and afraid, they stopped beside a stream to drink and eat some of the dried fruit. Clothes rumpled from sleep, they perched on a dead log and sat in silence for a while.

Karl ruffled his hair, trying to rid it of the clinging bits of hay, then put his cap on. Absently, he fingered the brim where the precious gold coins lay hidden.

"Franz, I just can't understand," Karl sighed, finally baring his thoughts. "*I* didn't kill Christ!"

Franz wiped a grimy hand over his face, wishing for a bath. "It's ignorance," he stated flatly. "It's true that the Jews rejected Christ, but no one took His life." Karl gave him a baffled look and Franz hurried on. "Jesus *gave* His life. Why, Karl, He was born just so He could die for our sins. If He hadn't died, then no one could be saved. Besides, people who call Jews 'Christ-killers' don't love Him. If they did, they would love the Jews, because Christ was a Jew!"

"But the people who persecute us say they are Christians!" Karl argued. "The German soldiers have *Gott mit uns* on their belt buckles. *God with us.*"

Franz moved when a ray of sunlight struck his eyes. "They aren't Christians, Karl. They only know *about* Christ; they don't know Him." Franz gazed into Karl's puzzled brown eyes. "Like I said, Christ was a Jew, so if they knew Him, how could they hate other Jews?? He smiled and decided to sound Jewish himself. "I ask you, does that make sense or are they *meshuggener* (crazy)? Such a world to live in!"

Karl tried on a weak smile. "You should be so smart! True? Of course true."

"So let us Jews be on our way, already."

They trudged forward, keeping on the move, going nowhere, knowing no one. Always on the alert lest they meet German soldiers prowling around the woods looking for Jews. Once they heard the faraway stutter of machine gun fire and quickly crouched behind some brush until it stopped. The last thing either of them needed was to be struck down by a stray bullet.

At times they were surrounded by rolling green hills. Other times they removed their shoes and socks to wade through icy streams. They tried to fill their shrunken stomachs with water but the rumbling was always there. Finally they gave up and ate the rest of the fruit.

"If we were in Poland, Franz mused, "we could try and make it back to my house to see if anyone is still there." He spread his hands. "But we're not in Poland. Not anymore."

Karl reached out suddenly as a warning for Franz to stop. "Look, we're coming to a village!"

Sure enough, a narrow, muddy road opened before them. Upon it a horse and wagon clattered into view. The youths shrank back out of sight and let it pass. It was loaded with produce, on its way to market. The horse was bony and looked tired. Its harness jingled and its hooves click-clacked listlessly as it tried to pull its heavy load to market.

Once it was past them, the fellows stepped onto the road and headed in the same direction.

"This is too risky," Karl worried. "You have German papers, but I'm a dead giveaway. If you're going into the village, then I'll have to hide someplace."

Franz motioned Karl to slip into the trees once more. Removing the small scissors from the rucksack, he slit the seam of his coat and took out the German marks.

"I'm going to buy us some food, Karl." Franz was about to suggest the other boy remain hidden in the woods, when the sound of harsh voices reached them.

"Karl!" Franz hissed. "Come on! *Hurry!*"

Across the narrow dirt road was a small bombed-out building that had probably been used for storage. They sprinted toward it on silent feet, not speaking again. Four German soldiers emerged from the woods scant seconds after the boys dove into the scarred shell.

Wildly, their eyes searched for a hiding place. One entire side of the structure had been blown away and most of the roof. What remained was blackened from fire and smoke. Above them was what was left of a loft. Leaning awkwardly against it was a wobbly-looking ladder.

Their glances locked and they nodded in quick understanding. All too fast the sound of heavy boots thudded toward them.

Karl bolted up the ladder. Franz was right behind him, his long legs taking the rungs two at a time.

Straw was strewn around the loft. It was dark and old and smelled like rat droppings and mold. A mouse scurried away as the boys sprawled out flat and tried not to breathe.

The voices came closer. The boys waited for the sounds to fade as the soldiers went on into town, but to their horror this did not happen. A couple of the men entered the shell of building to look around and rest. The other two sat in what remained of the doorway. The acrid smell of cigarette smoke drifted into the loft, and for one paralyzing moment Karl thought he was going to sneeze.

No! Franz mouthed the mouth and gestured for Karl to place a finger under his nose. Karl's olive face was red and he looked as though he might explode. Nose twitching, he followed Franz's suggestion and put a finger beneath his nose. *Please God, don't let me sneeze!*

The German soldiers stayed there for twenty minutes, leisurely smoking and talking. Though Franz knew perfectly what they were saying, Karl picked up only words now and then.

"Filthy Jews!" one of them spat out. "I know there's a nest of them hiding in the woods, but where are they?" He sounded frustrated and angry. "They must have dug a cave some where!"

"Don't worry, Helmut," another comforted, "it's only a matter of time until we find them." He roared with laughter. "When we do . . . rat-a-tat-tat!"

"Ach, the swine!" another soldier chimed in. "I say we march them to Hitler's ovens. Shooting is too good for them!"

Franz wanted to drop to the floor and take them all on at once, when the words of Jesus from the cross leapt into his mind.

Father, forgive them; they know not what they do.

But Franz was not Jesus and it was hard for him to forgive such monsters. Sure, he knew that Jesus had died for even Hitler's sins! Still, hearing what these soldiers were saying made him want to strike out. He was hurt and angry for Karl, and he felt glad that the Jewish boy could not understand all the soldiers were saying. A look in the gentle brown eyes, though, told Franz that Karl had understood enough.

The boys did not move an inch the entire time the soldiers were there. Once Franz got a cramp in the calf of his leg and struggled against reaching down to massage it. He dare not. They wondered if simply the sound of their breathing would not give away their presence. Their hearts thudded with terror. Surely the men below could hear the savage thundering of their pulses!

At long last the Germans stood and stretched lazily.

"Let's head for the village so we can get something to eat," one of them suggested.

"I think I'll just take a minute to take a look up there in the loft," another mumbled.

Hitler's Youth

"Forget it, you idiot!" a voice snapped peevishly. "We haven't heard so much as a mouse up there. No one could remain quiet this long!"

"You never know," the first soldier declared stubbornly. "I'm going to have a look."

"Suit yourself. We're going to find something to eat."

Franz and Karl stiffened. The muscle in Franz's calf was bunched up hard and painful. Both youths stopped breathing.

The sound of boots died away the same time feet began clunking up the ladder.

Jesus, protect us! Franz cried silently.

Hide me under the shadow of thy wings, Karl prayed.

They watched in terror as the top of a bucket helmet appeared. Then a sliver of a man's forehead. Karl closed his eyes against this unfolding horror.

At that moment a strange thing happened. The weak, charred ladder gave away and the soldier collapsed backwards to the concrete floor. His breath exploded and he cried out in surprise. Then, standing and dusting himself off with angry swipes of his hands, he stormed from the bombed-out building and went to catch up with his comrades.

At last Franz could pull up his tormented leg and rub away the cramp. "Thank You, God," he whispered.

"Yes, thank You, God," Karl echoed. But he knew that somehow Franz's words held an intimacy Karl knew nothing about.

Pulling some German marks from his pocket, Franz took time to count them and double check his papers. Now if he could only pull this off.

"You stay here, Karl. I'll buy us some food and then we'll duck back into the woods."

"But they're looking for Jews there too, Franz," Karl reminded him. Franz's sigh was ragged. "It's safer than here, maybe. Anyway, if we run into the Jews and they've found a safe hiding place, maybe we could join them."

"Maybe," Karl reluctantly agreed. "But we had better wait till dark to go back into the woods." He hesitated and sighed. "Franz, I hate this!"

Franz nodded grimly. "So do I, but we're still alive, aren't we? And we're going to stay alive, too . . . somehow. Just look what God did for us a moment ago."

"I know," Karl agreed softly. "Go ahead into the village, Franz, but . . . please come back."

Franz mustered up a smile he did not feel. "I wouldn't want to be alone in this crazy mixed-up world anymore than you, Karl."

Franz dropped easily to the floor and began walking toward the village. He was a tall, lonely figure, trying hard to be brave, trying to appear casual. Dogs barked and challenged him as he approached. Still he walked forward.

Karl watched through a small hole in the section of the wall that had been blown away. It was the loneliest and most frightening time of his life. What if Franz was arrested? What if the SS checked up on him and found out he was wanted for hiding Jews? Worse still, what if Franz changed his mind and walked out on him? He did, after all, have copies of his old identification papers.

As Franz neared the village, the muddy road turned into a cobblestone street. He saw at once that it was market day, for a large number of horses and wagons were present. Stalls had been set up around the village square where farmers brought produce and other wares for sale.

Franz frowned darkly when he saw that one woman had shoes and other items of clothing for sale. Had they been taken from some dead Jew discovered along the road? He hurried on.

He noted also that there were several German soldiers in the village. Some dove into a tiny cafe to eat cheese blintzes and drink coffee. Others lounged around looking for trouble. A few purchased food in the stalls.

"Well, young man," a voice snapped irritably, "do you want to buy something or not?"

Franz came to himself with a start and found that he was staring at the produce a farm woman had to offer. The last thing in the world he needed was to draw attention to himself and here he was daydreaming!

He purchased a loaf of black bread, a chunk of cheese, two apples, and a few potatoes. Without seeming to hurry, he strolled over to a grassy spot and sat down as though to eat.

Please, God, don't let anyone pay attention to me when I leave the village!

He munched on an apple, but the thought of real food was overwhelming and his stomach screamed for the bread and cheese.

After a little while he casually stood up, stretched, glanced around, and finally sauntered back down the road, leaving the village behind.

His heart was pumping hard, his pulses racing. Too many were German soldiers around to suit him, and it only took one to demand his papers and take him away.

He cast a wild look back toward the village. Distant voices could hardly be heard now. People haggling over prices. Customers demanding they pay less, sellers demanding they pay more.

No one was looking down the road. Franz slipped quietly inside the building. "Pssst! Karl!"

He heard a slight stirring from above. "Come on, the soldiers are all in the village eating. No one is paying any attention."

Karl forgot about the broken ladder and nearly fell from the loft. "You sure it's all right?"

Franz nodded and took another look outside. "Let's get back into the woods. It's safer than it is here."

"Did you get food?"

"Enough to last two or three days. And now that we know a village is so close, I can go back for more when we need it."

Karl put on his cap and assured himself that the three gold coins were safely in the brim. "Did anyone ask questions?"

"No. Everybody was busy trying to make sales. It's market day and people are too interested in making money to bother about a strange German boy."

The sun was already growing low on the horizon when they at last stopped beside a stream to eat.

Franz shoved a bite of bread into one cheek. "The next time I go into a village, though, I'm going to put on my other clothes. I'm so filthy and tattered people could get suspicious."

"Franz?" Karl had his head down, staring at his feet. "I was afraid you wouldn't come back."

Franz stared at his companion. "*Why?*"

Karl shrugged and looked embarrassed now that the truth was out. "You're an Aryan. Maybe you could get by the soldiers all right."

Franz shook his head and the stubborn lock of hair fell over his eye. He shoved it back impatiently. "I would never do that, Karl. I was arrested, too, remember? How long do you think it would take for the Germans to find out that I was a conspirator who hid Jews?" His hair fell down again. He ignored it and grinned wryly. "We're in this together, Karl. *Gefangenes* in hiding. Prisoners on the run. Anyway, where could I go? Our home in Germany is gone."

"I know. I just thought. . . ."

Franz poked Karl's shoulder. "Forget it, you're stuck with me. Jews to the end!"

Days crawled by. Afraid of arousing suspicion in the village, they went on and sought out another, smaller one. They slept in haystacks, abandoned buildings, lofts, anyplace that offered them shelter.

Nights were growing cold now and they often wakened to a gray drizzle. The wind blew, ghostly winds that spiraled around them and crept through their coats. Leaves crunched beneath their feet and pine needles shot from the trees like hail. Their breath white and frosty in the crisp air, they longed only for shelter; but some nights were spent in the open, where stars hung like chips of ice against the black dome of heaven.

Karl's black curly hair was snarled in spite of his efforts to keep it combed. Franz, too, was badly in need of a haircut. A shaggy blond mane, his hair hung over his ears and collar. The tiny mirror told him he was starting to look like a girl.

In the daytime they warmed themselves beside a small fire and roasted either corn or potatoes. They ate bread and cheese, but they longed for pierogies with sour cream and cheese blintzes and apple strudel.

Karl shivered beside their tiny, snapping fire. "Franz, we can't spend the winter in the woods!"

Franz examined his filthy hands and nails. "I'm going to try and find work, Karl. The next farm we come to, I'll see if they need help."

Karl frowned. His brown eyes held a world of questions. "And be kicked out like last time?"

"We'll pray that God leads us to just the right one. A farm where they'll hide you while I work."

Karl gazed at Franz sadly. "You're a dreamer."

"Maybe not. It might not be so possible in Poland, but we're not in Poland. I'm telling you, Karl, a lot of the German people hate what's happening and want to help your people."

Karl's frown deepened, still unsure about Franz's plan.

The first light snow fell the first of October. A cold weak sun soon melted it, but the youths knew that their position was perilous.

Franz walked into the village on market day to purchase food, leaving Karl alone in the woods. When he returned, he was astonished to find Karl wearing his yarmulke and rocking back and forth. When it struck Franz what was happening, he tried to quietly backtrack.

"Yom Kippur," he whispered. "The Day of Atonement, when Jews confess their sins."

Franz's foot came down on a dry twig that snapped beneath his foot. Alerted, Karl whirled to face his companion.

"I-I'm sorry," Franz stammered lamely. "I didn't mean to . . . I forgot what day it is."

The boys had carefully kept track of time since they had been on the run. Yet, though Franz had been present on this special day before, when his home had been occupied by Jews, he had somehow forgotten.

"It's all right." Karl stopped weaving back and forth and removed his skullcap, which he carefully folded and put back in his pocket. "I've already confessed every sin I can think of."

Franz smiled, wishing Karl knew Messiah Jesus, who forgave and then forgot about one's sins. Wished that Karl would not look backwards to the old animal sacrifices but could understand that it was now the blood of *the* Lamb of God, Jesus, who had shed *His* blood for the forgiveness of sin.

"Let's go look for a friendly farm," he suggested.

Trees were thick where they were and there was a lot of dry brush. They were about to walk over to a stream to eat when they heard a sound. Franz craned his neck to see what it was, and his skin began to prickle. With horror, he saw tan uniforms coming toward them.

"Get down!" he hissed. "Karl, *hide!*"

Karl stood paralyzed seconds before four arrogant Hitler's Youth came into view.

Shot!

Karl stood as if turned to stone, and Franz's thoughts were whirling. In a simple gesture he stuck out an arm and knocked Karl into the brush, where he lay without moving. Then, gulping in a deep breath, he stepped out into the direct path of the Youth. Throwing an arm high into the air he made a meaningless sound.

The uniformed boys stopped, stunned by the swift appearance of another human being. Their own arms shot up, palms outward. In unison they shouted, "Heil Hitler!"

Franz would have passed them by, but the Youth reconsidered the strange presence of the blond boy. Their cold blue eyes took in his tattered appearance and long hair. There was a hurried conference and one of them shouted, "*Hande hoch!*"

Franz obeyed instantly and thrust both hands into the air.

Hitler's Youth turned on him like a pack of wild dogs, shoving him around, yelling in his face, demanding his papers.

Franz dug out his papers and prayed they would pass inspection. "I'm in a hurry," he tried to explain.

"Where are you going?" one of them charged.

"To a farm. To work."

The icy blue eyes grew cunning. "Why don't you come with us? Join the Youth? Do something great with your life?"

"I can't. I have to work."

"If you joined Hitler's Youth," one of them suggested, "you could wear a clean, sharp uniform." Proudly he stroked his own spotless uniform. "And you'd get your hair cut so you wouldn't look like a girl!"

Franz returned the papers to his pocket. He already knew how he looked in comparison to these spit-polished boys beside him. Only their boots were dusty from the floor of the forest.

"I have to go," Franz said, and lifted his chin a little. Then, with another smart salute and another mumble, he began to walk away.

Instantly the Youth raised their own arms and cried, "Heil Hitler!"

Franz felt a little smug that he had fooled them on that at least; for not for a thousand worlds was he going to salute Hitler!

He walked slowly, casually, and could sense the eyes of the four Youth following him. He knew that they could easily have tripped over Karl lying motionless in the brush almost at their feet. As it was, one boy nearly tripped over him as he walked away.

Franz did not stop until he was sure the four Youth were out of sight. Then, almost in a panic, he darted back the way he had come.

"Karl," he whispered urgently, "they're gone! You can come out!"

There was a rustling noise as Karl backed slowly from the brush. With a ragged sigh he stood trembling beside Franz. "One of them almost tripped over me!"

Franz looked grim. "I saw him. Come on, we have to get out of here!"

"If there are any other Jews hiding in the woods, I wish we could find them," Karl said wistfully.

Franz sighed. "Maybe it's better that we can't. A lot of people together would be easier to find than just two."

Karl nodded and shrugged. "I guess so. Franz, if you hadn't come back when you did, they would have caught me."

Franz did not answer. He thought he had heard a slight sound behind them. No twigs had snapped. There had been no voices. No sound of feet crunching through dead leaves. Yet. . . .

Silently he slipped behind a clump of trees and motioned for Karl to follow. They waited in utter quiet for what seemed like an eternity.

"What?" Karl mouthed the word.

Franz squinted and shook his head. A mummy stillness lay over the woods. Maybe, Franz decided, it had been his imagination. Still, he could sense that they were not alone. What, then?

He peered around the trees and his neck hairs began to prickle. Tan uniforms creeping toward them. Rifles held in front of the Youth.

Dear Jesus!

Hitler's Youth had not left the area at all. Suspicious and wary, they had doubled back.

"*Jews!*" one of them yelled suddenly.

The cry sent Karl and Franz bolting headlong for a place to hide. Speeding through the trees, they leaped over rocks and brush and crashed through cold, bubbling streams. Hitler's Youth were hot on their trail. Gunfire rattled and bullets began singing through the air around the fleeing boys. The Youth had been trained well and were sharp-shooters. So far, the only thing saving Franz and his companion was the fact that they were moving and harder to hit.

"Come on," someone yelled furiously, "let's get them!"

Yes, Franz thought balefully, killing us would be a feather in their caps so far as the Fuhrer was concerned. It would probably mean decorations for them. Medals for honor and bravery.

Not hesitating in their headlong flight, Karl and Franz came dripping and cold from a deep stream, only to see a river dead ahead. Behind them, the four Youth crashed through the woods, straining to get Franz and Karl in their sights.

Bullets flew around them. Some struck the trees with a solid thump. Others hit the water, exploding it around them. Suddenly Karl jerked. "Franz! I've been hit!"

"No!" Franz cried in desperation. "No, Karl!" Karl had a glazed look in his brown eyes. A strange, empty look. His face was white, and the icy water was turning crimson.

GRETA HANSSLER

There was a triumphant yell behind them. "We got 'em!"

The murky brown water deepened and Karl was not able to use his arm to swim. His head went under. Bubbles of air came to the surface and burst. Franz gazed about him desperately.

"Come on! Hurry! We'll finish them off!"

"Juden!" yelled another of Hitler's Youth. "Get the dirty Jews!"

"The blond Jew had papers, can you believe it!" shouted another, his voice filled with fury. "He almost had me fooled!"

Franz pulled Karl's head above water, but he was not strong enough to tow him to the other side. It would have been hopeless anyway, with the other boys so close. He saw but one possibility. There was a large tree on the bank of the river, and its roots formed an empty black space over the water. If he could just get Karl that far, maybe. . . .

Karl was slightly shorter than Franz's five-eight and could not touch bottom. His body swayed awkwardly in the icy river, and his water-logged coat made the going even harder.

"Where are they?" demanded someone approaching the bank.

With his remaining strength Franz towed his burden beneath the giant black tree roots. It was slimy but roomy, and fish darted away from them as they pressed as far back as possible.

Feet pounded along the riverbank. Bullets splatted the water where Franz and Karl had stood seconds before.

"Where did they go?" someone asked in frustration.

"Can't you see?" snarled another. "Look at the water. That's blood you're looking at. We got them already."

Cheers, congratulations and back-slapping followed. Then one boy fired off a few more rounds just to make sure.

"Cut it out, Boris, you're wasting ammunition. They'll wash up somewhere down river."

Franz thought they would never leave. Brown water filled with green slime and bits of bark floated around their chins. Both of them were freezing cold and Karl was beginning to moan.

"Come on," one of the Youth finally decided, "let's go report this incident."

"Ja!" agreed another. "The Fuhrer will be proud of us!"

Still they hesitated, scanning the river for sign of bodies. Then at last they turned and walked away. Their excited voices died out slowly, and at long last the woods were quiet again.

"Hang on, Karl, we have to get out of here."

Karl clenched his teeth against the raw pain snaking through his left shoulder. "I don't know if I can."

"You have to."

Franz eased his friend through the grappling roots and pulled him backwards to the bank of the river. "Can you touch bottom?" Franz panted.

"I-I think so." White and shaking uncontrollably, Karl thought perhaps he was about to faint. "I can touch . . . barely."

We're in Your hands, Lord. Help us.

The bank was slick with mud as Franz half dragged Karl out of the water. They were dripping and freezing cold and their teeth were chattering wildly. Franz knew he dared not make a fire, not with Hitler's Youth around. And Karl was in shock and half unconscious.

The sun died in a mass of heavy gray clouds that seemed to have scudded in from out of nowhere. The night would be black and bitterly cold. Already their breath hung frosty white on the chill air.

"I can't carry you, Karl, you have to walk. Come on, you can do it." Franz kept talking and tried to make Karl talk too. They had to keep their heads or all would be lost.

"So c-cold," Karl gasped. "P-pain is so bad."

"You can do it, Karl, one foot after the other. That's it. Come on now, talk to me."

Karl stumbled and would have fallen if Franz had not grabbed his soaking coat.

"You have to keep walking, Karl, or we'll both freeze."

Karl cried out in pain. "I c-can't, Franz!"

"You have to."

A broken moon hung in the black sky above them, and one brave star hovered on the horizon.

Franz squinted. Wait a minute. That's wasn't a star; it was the yellow glow of a naphtha lamp burning in a window somewhere!

"I think there's a house just ahead, Karl! Do you see the light?"

Before Karl could reply there came the familiar sound of a dog barking. A moment later the animal rushed at them from out of the darkness, a big white creature with amber eyes and a wet, black nose that poked against Franz questioningly.

"Come on, boy, it's all right."

Karl's coat was soaked with blood by the time they stumbled to the door of the small farmhouse. He was moaning in agony when the door opened and they faced a cautious farm woman. Her hair was gray and wispy, pulled back into a knot at the back of her head. Her blue eyes were wary and she kept a hand on the neck of her dog.

"Ja? And what would you be wantin'?"

"Please," Franz pleaded, "we need help. My friend has been hurt and we're wet and cold. We don't mean you any harm. Please."

She surveyed them a moment longer before sighing and opening the door to let them come in. "You fell into the river?" she asked, astonished that this would happen.

"It's a long story," Franz told her. "My friend is hurt."

The woman saw the blood now and clucked her tongue in concern and sympathy. Quickly she helped Franz peel off Karl's coat and shirt. Her gentle calloused fingers explored the bullet wound.

"It went in the soft part of the shoulder," she explained, "and it came out the back. It will heal all right."

Getting a clean cloth and some warm water, she bathed the wound and bandaged it. Then she gestured toward another room. "I laid out dry clothes for you. Quickly or you will catch your death!" When they hesitated, she gestured again. "The clothes belonged to my husband, may he rest in peace. Hurry now, before you both catch pneumonia."

Franz wanted to fall down and kiss her feet.

A few minutes later the boys emerged from the woman's bedroom, clean and dry and warm. Karl was in pain but trying to be courageous.

"Sit down and have some hot food. You are hungry, eh?"

"Awfully hungry," Franz said. "I had bought some food in the village, but it was lost in the river."

"So you are Jewish boys on the run, eh?"

The smell of food was intoxicating and they sat down at the table obediently.

"Franz is not Jewish," Karl explained in his hesitant German.

"My family hid Jews," Franz said, "and one night the SS broke in and we were arrested."

"Ach, that Hitler!" the woman said, shaking her head in disdain. "It is the same story everywhere."

Her plump form turned back to the stove and a moment later she placed steaming bowls of thick, savory potato soup and slices of black bread and butter before the starving youths. Not yet finished, she poured them large cups of boiling black coffee. "To warm you," she told them, then sat down at the table with them. When Karl groaned, she hastened to say, "I am sorry there is nothing for the pain."

Karl managed a tight smile. "I'll be all right."

She squeezed his hand. "Of course you will! You Jews are going through terrible things these days, so what is a little pain, eh? But you did not tell me how you got shot."

Franz jerked his head toward the woods. "Hitler's Youth."

"Ach, a bad lot, those!" The woman stroked back a wisp of hair and rubbed her rough red cheek. "We should get acquainted, ja? My name is Greta Hanssler. And you?"

Franz smiled. "My friend is Karl Rosenthal and I'm Franz Bedke. Mrs. Hanssler? Thank you for helping us."

"Well, when that brute dog of mine didn't attack you, I knew you were just two boys in trouble."

Franz gazed at the huge white animal snoozing peacefully in front of the stove. Hearing the word "brute" he lifted one lazy eyelid to peer at them, then sighed and went back to sleep.

"What do you plan to do when you leave here?" Greta Hanssler asked suddenly.

The soup suddenly lost its flavor. Outside, the night was black and the clouds had swarmed over the moon like bees over a hive. Franz tried to swallow but the soup and bread stuck in his throat. Quickly he swallowed some coffee.

"I—we don't know. I want to find work on some farm where Karl can hide until all the craziness is over."

Greta sighed again and folded her calloused hands on the table. "Why does it have to be *some* farm? Why not this farm? I've needed help ever since my husband died two years ago. And my son. . . ." Her blue eyes clouded over. "I'm not sure where he is or when he will be coming home."

Karl was still moaning and shaking as he tried to eat. Now he turned questioning eyes upon Franz.

"She wants us to stay here," Franz translated joyfully.

"The only problem," Greta continued gravely, "is that you don't look too strong."

"But I am!" Franz cried. "It's just that I've lost so much weight from being hungry all the time." His eyes were pleading. "If you'll just give me a chance!"

Greta still appeared hesitant. "There is another problem. You see . . . I can't pay you. All I can do is give you good food and a place to sleep." Her thin lips parted in a rueful smile. "And see that you both have clean, dry clothes to wear."

"That's enough!" Franz cried. "It's all we ask!"

A twinkle came into the keen blue eyes. "Can you milk a cow?"

"Well . . . no," Franz admitted reluctantly. "But I can learn!"

Hungry as he was, Karl had trouble eating. The pain was nagging away at him, and he was pale and dizzy.

"Ach!" Greta scooped away his bowl of soup. "You can have it later. Come." And she helped him stand. Leading him to a cot near the crackling fire, she helped him down and covered him with a blanket. "Try to sleep. The wound is not bad and you will feel better tomorrow."

Franz wondered how many gunshot wounds she had treated but decided not to ask, since she seemed to know what she was doing.

The woman was bustling around the room making a bed for Franz. Pausing at last, she stood with her calloused hands on her hips. "Now then, you will both sleep down here tonight where it's warm, ja? Then you must hide up in the loft until I can spread word in the village that I have taken a boy to help me." She glanced at the moaning Karl and wagged her head. "Karl, of course, must stay hidden until. . . ." She shrugged and did not finish her thought.

For the first time in months Franz felt full and warm and safe. "We used to live in Germany," Franz explained shortly, "so I have papers. Unless someone checks out my family it shouldn't be any trouble."

Mrs. Hanssler pondered for a moment. "We will always have to be careful. German soldiers are everywhere." She busied herself washing the soup bowls. "The SS. . . ." She shook her head. "Ach, they seem to know everything."

The Goyim Bible

During the weeks that followed, Franz learned not only how to milk and care for Greta's three cows, he learned how to separate the cream and get all of it ready for market.

Greta had woven the news of her farm help through the village carefully, so that when Franz made appearances it was no surprise to anyone.

He could now harness the mare alone, and on market day he piled the wagon high with root vegetables, milk and eggs and drove into the village to set up a stall on the tiny square. Mrs. Hanssler had also taught him to be a careful trader. Carrots for naphtha for the lamps. Potatoes for coal for the hungry stove. Two pints of cream for a shirt or a piece of cloth for Greta an apron.

Then, weary from a long day of selling and haggling, he would leave the cobblestone streets and return to what was now home.

Far from cities and large villages, there were few soldiers about. When there were, they, like the village people, accepted the fact that Franz was one of them.

Winter was brutal. Snowy and bitterly cold. Franz tended the animals and made small repairs around the house. Karl stayed down where it was warm during the day, but at night both boys slept in the loft. If a neighbor came to the door, Karl sometimes remained in the loft for hours.

"I'm going crazy in the loft with nothing to do!" Karl grumbled to Franz. "There isn't even anything to read!"

"I have my Polish Bible," Franz offered.

The precious contents of the rucksack had barely been saved that terrible day when Karl had been shot. Though Mrs. Hanssler had a Bible, Franz would have hated to borrow it, for she was often immersed in it herself.

"Your Bible is a Gentile Bible!" Karl protested.

Franz shook his head and the stubborn lock of hair fell over his eye. "The Old Testament is just like yours, Karl. All the same people are there. Moses, Elijah, David, Isaiah. . . ."

Karl's shoulder had healed rapidly and he was grumpy and discontented from being inside all the time. "I suppose I can read it then." His dark eyes begged Franz. "I just want to get out, go into the village, take a walk! I can't stand being cooped up all the time!"

"It's hard, I know," Franz sympathized. "How about if we go for a walk tonight after it gets dark?"

Karl looked like a wistful child. "Could we? It would great just to walk through the fields."

Franz nodded and handed Karl his Bible. "I have to get back to work, but I'll be back as soon as I can."

While Franz spent the afternoon tending the animals and cleaning the barn, Karl browsed through the pages of the Old Testament.

"What a good time for Messiah to come," he mused softly.

With that thought in mind, he began to explore the prophecies about the Messiah. Karl had learned the Scriptures well, both in Jewish school and by his father, but he was still surprised to discover that this Goyim Bible was exactly like his Jewish Bible. He still wasn't sure why Gentiles loved the Old Testament.

"Messiah . . ." Karl's whisper caressed the word. "Born of a virgin . . . born in Bethlehem . . . riding into Jerusalem on a donkey . . . rejected. . . ." He resisted the terrible temptation to look within the pages of the mysterious New Testament.

They ate pierogies with pork gravy for supper. Karl knew, of course, that it wasn't kosher, but Mrs. Hanssler was kind to them and he could not hurt her by refusing her food. Besides, his father had always said that the Eternal was merciful and understanding.

"I promised Karl a walk tonight, Mrs. Hanssler," Franz said when they finished eating. "Just across the fields. We won't be gone long."

Greta Hanssler bit her lip. "Be careful, especially when you come back. Ach, not that I'm expecting company on a night as cold as this, but. . . ." Her wrinkled face fell into a smile. "I don't want anything to happen to my boys."

When the boys were outside, Karl said gently, "For a Gentile, Mrs. Hanssler is all right!"

Franz laughed. "I'm a Gentile! Am I all right?"

Karl slapped Franz on the back. "You're almost as Jewish as I am, already!"

Stars were bright overhead, and cold. There wasn't a cloud in the sky and the moon sprayed the world with light. Their breath came in white clouds as they picked their way over the stubble of a corn field. Far away a dog heard their approach and gave a warning bark.

"You were right," Karl murmured, ducking his chin into the warmth of the wool scarf Greta had given him. "Your Bible is the same as ours."

Franz glanced over at him. "What did you read?"

"I read some of the prophecies about the Messiah."

Franz arched his blond brows. "Really? I love the prophecies too, Karl. I especially love the way they're all fulfilled in the New Testament."

Karl gave him a sharp look but did not answer.

"That dog sounds a little too close," Franz told his companion. "Maybe we should turn back."

Karl sighed and stood for a moment looking at the stars. "I guess so. But only on the condition that we do it again."

Franz grinned. "Sure."

"Franz? Do you think about your family a lot? Wondering where they are and what happened to them?"

Sadness entered the blue eyes. "All the time."

"Me too. Especially Sonia, with her being so blond and all."

"I know, Karl," Franz said softly. "All we can do is pray for them."

Karl tripped over some stubble. "I do that too. A lot."

Off and on all that night Karl wakened to puzzle over what Franz had said about the Messiah being in the Gentile Bible. By the time Franz had gone off to milk the cows, curiosity had him in its grip. Opening the Bible, he began to read.

"But this is crazy!" he muttered to himself. "It can't be right! This says that—that Jesus was born of a virgin! That—that He was born in . . . Bethlehem!" The word exploded in his mind. The prophet Micah had said, *But thou Bethlehem, though thou be little among the thousands of Judah, yet out of thee shall he come forth unto me that is to be ruler in Israel.*

Reading on, he found that Jesus had ridden into Jerusalem on a donkey as the prophet Zechariah had written.

"I know my people hate Jesus because they've been so persecuted by people who claimed to be Christians," Karl told himself. "But He was a *Jew!* And He was kind and good!" As he read on, Karl realized that he loved this man called Jesus.

May Jesus Christ protect you.

Mr. Wrona. Yes, Karl remembered. The words had been confusing at the time but slowly he was beginning to understand.

Then he came to the part about the crucifixion and Karl was stunned. How could they do something so horrible to someone who was so good?

Rage boiled up inside his heart. *How could they?* It was awful. Terrible! Closing the Bible where they were nailing Jesus to the cross, he flung it against the wall. So there was no hope after all! They had killed Jesus Christ, the Jew, just like they were killing Jews that very day. Well, he wanted nothing more to do with this awful Goyim Bible!

Stranger in the House

Winter unleashed its fury on the small farm. Heavy snows and deep drifts shut them in for two weeks. Howling winds roared down the chimney and sobbed around the house like a lost child. With the danger of soldiers prowling around nearly zero, Karl was able to come outdoors and help Franz with the work of feeding the animals, splitting wood and shoveling snow. On one cold December night the boys helped Greta Hanssler deliver a new baby calf, then hurried to dry it off and get it warm.

Christmas arrived, along with the eight days of Hanukkah. There were no presents, though Karl and Franz did cut down a tree. The three people in the small house dutifully trimmed it with strings of popcorn and bits of cotton. Karl recounted for them the story of Hanukkah, though Franz had heard it several times.

"Hanukkah celebrates a Jewish victory and the rededication of the temple," Karl told them eagerly. "The altar light was supposed to always be kept burning, but everything had been destroyed. That's when one drop of oil was finally discovered, and it burned for eight days and nights until more oil was found." His eyes shone. "At home we always sing songs, exchange gifts, and light another candle through all the eight days of Hanukkah."

"Not this year," Franz said sadly. "But we have a Christmas tree!"

"No, it's a Hanukkah tree!" Karl declared mischievously.

"And we have a Gift," Mrs. Hanssler said. "We have Jesus."

A slow depression crept over Karl. He thought about the prophecies. Even Zechariah said that one day the Jews would look upon Him whom they had pierced and would mourn for Him. *Pierced!* Jesus Christ had been pierced. Would his people wake up one day and mourn because they had rejected the One they had waited for so long? For surely all the Old Testament prophecies pointed to Yeshua. Jesus, the Messiah.

"And tomorrow we shall celebrate!" Greta Hanssler cried good-naturedly. "We shall have cheese blintes and apple strudel!"

"That really sounds good, Mrs. Hanssler!" Franz sobered quickly, looked thoughtful, and finally said with grim humor, "And tomorrow I will be fifteen years old."

"A real Christmas present you were, ja? Well, I am sorry you can't be home with your family. They would have had a great celebration, no?"

Franz nodded and looked away. Home. Family. Where were they now? It had been so long. They seemed to belong to some other time.

Greta was not having an easy time of it either. She had not seen her son Johann for two years. Was he dead or alive? Surely, God forbid, he had not turned his back on his teaching about God and become a part of Hitler's army!

Karl could not bear to think of his own family. Slipping on a coat that had once belonged to Mr. Hanssler, he went outside to feed the chickens.

That night Greta managed to scrape together enough sugar to make a small batch of taffy. Putting aside their fears and their longings, they made a game of pulling the hot sticky mass until it thickened into strips. Then they sat at the table and ate it with cups of steaming tea.

Determined to get into the spirit of things, Franz and Greta sang Christmas carols. Karl listened first in curiosity, then in wonder.

" . . . Round yon virgin, mother and child. . . . "

A virgin. Karl swallowed. Isaiah had said, "A virgin shall conceive and bear a son." Young Mary had been a virgin, so the New Testament declared.

" . . . Holy infant, so tender and mild. . . . "

Holy infant. The baby Jesus. Messiah. God had called Him Emmanuel.

He listened still as the others drifted into a song about the little town of Bethlehem. *But thou Bethlehem . . . out of thee shall come . . . he who is to be ruler in Israel.*

It was all beautiful. Mysterious. Haunting.

When there was a lull in the singing, though, Karl broke in sadly. "Why do you sing about someone who is dead? What good is a dead Messiah? If He is . . . the . . . Messiah."

Karl and Greta stared at one another in shocked wonder. Franz recalled picking up his Bible from the floor and gently straightening the crumpled pages. So Karl had read the New Testament after all!

"But, Karl, He is not dead!" Mrs. Hanssler cried warmly. She laid a hard, calloused hand over Karl's. "He is alive, son."

"No! No, He's not! I read it and they crucified Him! And He did only good for people. They didn't treat Him any better than they treat Jews today!"

"You must have stopped reading where Jesus was crucified," Greta murmured.

"Well, sure! I didn't want to read anymore."

"You missed the best part," Franz said, smiling. "It's true they killed Jesus, but, Karl, He didn't stay dead. He came back to life again!"

Karl's gentle brown eyes widened with hope and wonder. "He's alive?" he whispered.

Greta began leafing through her Bible. "Perhaps we should read it, no?"

Karl listened intently to the story of the resurrection, then mouthed the words softly, *"He is not here; he is risen."* A slow smile lit up his face. "But then, where is He?"

"In heaven," Franz told him, "and He's going to come back! We don't know when, but He is coming back!"

Karl tried to shake off the confusion. "There is so much I don't understand."

"Look at it this way," Mrs. Hanssler said. "What were the Old Testament sacrifices about? Why were they performed?"

Karl's eyes cleared instantly. This was something he understood. "Because their blood forgave sin."

"That's what the blood of Jesus does, Karl. He was God's Sacrifice for the sins of the world. Surely you must know that the old sacrifices all pointed to the true Sacrifice for sin?"

Karl nodded absently. Now, suddenly, he was beginning to understand. "And all the time," he muttered slowly, "the Jews hated Jesus Christ because people who claimed to know Him did such cruel things to us. And because . . . because they called us 'Christ-killers.' "

"Of course," Greta soothed. "But people who say they love Christ and hate Jews don't know the Saviour at all. Never forget that, Karl."

"Yeshua," Karl whispered. "Jesus, the Messiah. How could we have missed it for so long?"

Leaving the room, Karl walked out into the bitter cold. The snow had stopped and there was a quarter moon dangling from milky clouds. He gazed earnestly into the heavens.

Soon, he too would be fifteen years old, but he felt as if he wanted to cry. "Yeshua," he whispered brokenly. "I know that You are truly the Messiah. Please, I want to know You like Franz knows You. I want You real and close to me always."

He thought of being able to share this glorious news with his parents, but was stopped immediately. He would have to go slowly. He must be wise, for Karl knew that his father still regarded the very name of Jesus as something to be hated and feared. But God would help him and show him how and when to speak. He would be patient.

The long, harsh winter seemed to last forever. All the coal had been burned and wood was in short supply. The horse and cows stood in their stalls stomping and blowing. Several chickens froze to death. Franz and Karl walked into the woods behind the house and cut a tree to chop for wood.

Karl's birthday came and went, and Mrs. Hanssler somehow found the necessary items to again make cheese blintzes and apple strudel in celebration of this important event.

Though all three people in the little house bore great sorrow, still they found joy and peace in being together. They had learned to flow together like a family, and the boys never forgot that they owed Greta Hanssler their very lives.

And then one cold drizzly morning in early April, Franz wakened to the sound of voices drifting up from the kitchen.

A Ray of Hope

Franz grabbed Karl's shoulder just as he started to mumble something.

"Shhh! Someone's downstairs!"

Karl's smooth brow puckered in a frown as he sighed and struggled to wake up. "Who?"

Franz shook his head and stood to look through the high window. There was no car and no wagon, but a bicycle leaned against the spring house where Greta kept her root vegetables in the summer.

His knee cracked like a pistol shot when he lowered himself to the straw mattress, and for an endless moment they waited to see whether the sound had been heard below.

Soft laughter floated up to them. Franz smiled a knowing smile. So the visitor was someone Mrs. Hanssler knew. That wasn't as bad as the person being a soldier or a member of the SS!

Time dragged. One hour. Two. There was more laughter. Then the voices grew low and confidential. The boys did not move.

And suddenly, "Karl! Franz! Come on down, boys!"

The fellows looked at each other sharply. How could Greta asked Karl to come down? Surely she wouldn't turn them in now!

Resigned, they struggled into their trousers and climbed reluctantly down the ladder. A moment later they were standing before a tall stranger with thin brown hair, gray eyes and a craggy face. He was anything but handsome, yet he did not appear unkind. He was wearing camouflage clothing and looked tired and nervous.

Without speaking, he surveyed the boys, then sighed and went back to the kitchen, where coffee waited for him on the table.

"Come," Mrs. Hanssler said briskly. "I have your breakfast ready."

The boys sat stiff and unsure across from the man, not knowing how to act or what to say. Were they under arrest? The man could not take them away on a bicycle.

Mrs. Hanssler placed potato pancakes and fried bacon on their plates. "This is Karl," she told the stranger, "my Jewish boy. And this is Franz. He is German. But, ach, I told you that already."

The man stuck out a large, strong hand and the boys shook it hesitantly. Greta poured coffee all around, and joined them at the table.

Abruptly, the stranger's face cracked in a smile and Franz thought perhaps he did not smile very often. "My name is Johann," he told them, "and I appreciate the way you've taken care of my mother."

Karl swallowed but the food wouldn't go down. Hadn't Mrs. Hanssler feared that her son had joined forces with Hitler's henchmen? "Please, Yeshua," he prayed, and realized with a shock that he was talking to Jesus.

"You have nothing to fear from Johann," Greta assured them earnestly. "I know now what he has been up to, and thanks be to God he is not tied up with that Hitler bunch!"

Johann smiled once more. "I'm working with an underground movement to get Jews smuggled into Switzerland," he confided.

Karl gasped. "Is this possible?"

Johann nodded. "Tricky but possible. It's a slow and delicate business, and it's costly, but, yes, that's what we are doing."

Karl's thoughts snagged on the word *costly*. "I have some gold coins! Can you get us into Switzerland?"

Johann looked thoughtful. "Mother told me about all your problems." He sniffed and sighed. "It will take time, but . . . I may be able to help."

"Will we be able to go home after we get into Switzerland?" Franz asked. "That is . . . if we still have homes?"

Johann fingered his cup, sipped some coffee. "It may not be quite that simple. I'll need the names of your family members and your former addresses. Then I will contact the Red Cross in Switzerland to see if they can trace your families whereabouts."

"And if they can?" Karl asked eagerly.

"Then we will wait for a dark rainy night and hike to the border. You will have the name of a contact on the other side."

Dark rainy night. That put their journey somewhere in the future, for the ground was still covered with snow.

"How far is it?" Karl questioned, not caring much as long as he could be with his family again.

Johann jerked his head. "Fourteen kilometers. We can walk it easily and arrive at the border while it's still dark."

Franz leaned forward eagerly and nearly upset his coffee. "But won't there be guards?"

Johann nodded. "Guard. A very small crossing with one very greedy guard." He really grinned now and showed two rows of crooked white teeth. "That's where the money comes in. He knows now what we're up to, but he'll turn his head if money is involved."

The youths laughed, then instantly sobered. The sound was strange, for there had been so little to laugh about.

"Shall I get the gold coins now?"

Johann put up a hand. "Not yet. Wait until I come for you." He studied the boys closely. "I must warn you, these things don't happen overnight. We must plan each move carefully, and trust me when I say that there are Jews who are in really dangerous situations who must be smuggled across the frontier ahead of you."

The man smiled a twisted smile, stood, sighed deeply, and embraced his mother. "I must go."

Greta looked concerned. "Johann, you're so tired! Why not wait and leave tomorrow?"

"I wish I could, and, yes, I am tired. But a man and his wife are waiting to be taken across the border tonight. I can't fail them." He turned. "Boys, thank you for caring for my mother."

Franz smiled ruefully. "She's the one who has taken care of us!" he protested.

The man laid a hand on each of the youths' shoulders. "Be prepared to travel at a moment's notice, all right? Whatever you intend to take along, have it all ready in advance."

When Johann pedaled away, the boys were seized with both joy and fear. They were going to be reunited with their families!

Or . . . were they?

Trek to Freedom

Karl and Franz waited in an agony of anticipation from the moment Johann pedaled away from the farm.

"A week!" Karl guessed. "Two at the most!"

Franz frowned doubtfully. "I hope so, but . . . Karl, Mrs. Hanssler will need help getting her garden ready."

"Ach!" the woman snorted. "God sent *you*, didn't He? And He will also send someone else to help me." Her rough, work worn hands were busy peeling potatoes. "Besides, Johann will come home one day." Her bushy gray brows lifted hopefully. "Perhaps he will bring a bride, yes? That would be nice."

"You saved our lives," Karl said shyly, feeling awkward about expressing his feelings. "You are a good, kind Goy."

She laid a calloused hand on his cheek. "And you are a wonderful Jewish boy." She clucked her tongue. "And for you to have found your Messiah—! Ah, how good that is!"

Karl still got that odd stirring in his heart when he thought about it. "No one could ever make me believe that Yeshua is not Messiah." He sighed and looked thoughtful. "But I know that I must be careful how I share this news with my parents."

Greta nodded. "Ja. Wise like the serpent but gentle like the dove, eh? Now come, boys, we must talk."

The youths glanced at each other uneasily. The woman looked suddenly very sober and her tone was filled with warning. She poured tea and placed fresh bread and butter on the table.

When they were seated around the old wooden table, she began slowly. "Of course you are both excited about going home, and you should be." She studied them for a long time. "But you must realize that things will not be the same. For instance, Karl, your parents will not be in the ghetto. If they have been arrested, they could be . . . anywhere."

Franz thought the "anywhere" sounded a lot more like Dachau or Treblinka or Ravensbruck. He buttered a slice of bread to keep his hands busy and his eyes down.

Karl felt prickles of cold electricity race through him.

Greta went on doggedly, not liking this conversation anymore than the boys. "Franz, your parents *were* arrested." Her voice was sad and grim. "We must face facts, boys. Once you get into Switzerland, the Red Cross will take over, but. . . ." She looked away. "The truth is, neither of you may have a home to return to."

Nooo! The word screamed through Karl's mind. His parents had to be alive! Surely they had not been discovered and thrown into Hitler's furnaces! He had always seen them hidden away safe somewhere. A place where he could one day join them.

Franz felt numb and shaken. What Mrs. Hanssler said was true. His parents had been arrested. Maybe . . . *shot.*

"We will pray and trust," Greta was saying softly, "but it is better to be prepared, ja?"

"I guess so," Karl muttered. "And just to know! We have to know about our families."

Greta's red, dry face fell into the leathery folds of a smile. "Still, we will hope. God can work miracles today the same as when He rolled back the Rea Sea and fed the multitudes with a little bread and a few fish, eh?"

Franz scooted back his chair. He felt sick over Greta's words of caution. "We have to get busy, Karl."

After they had donned their jackets and were away from the house, Karl voiced his hopes. "Franz, our parents *could* be all right! Your mother and father may be out of prison and mine could have made it to safety."

A week passed. Three. A month. Days grew warm and the snow melted. Karl was forced to retreat back into the loft much of the time. The tattered rucksack was packed and waiting to be carried away.

Even the kind old woman grew anxious and started at every sound. "He will come," she sighed. "We must be patient."

If their parents *were* alive, Franz wondered ruefully if he and Karl would be recognized. Farm work had made them hard and muscled. Franz now stood at five-ten, with Karl right behind him at five-eight.

Now that warm weather had arrived, the ground was ready for plowing and planting. But Franz had no idea how to use the hand plow, and Greta's joints ached too badly to help. So the boys went out after dark and turned the soil by hand. It was hard work and made them too tired to lay awake listening for Johann's footfalls downstairs.

"I don't think he's coming for us," Karl announced dismally. "Something must have gone wrong."

"I hope not," Franz replied, biting his lip. The truth was, he too wondered about the man's long absence.

It was early fall when Johann appeared suddenly at the farm. He had brought dress material for his mother and, wonder of wonders, chocolate bars for the boys. It had now been a full year since the day Karl and Franz had fled for freedom under Hitler's prison train.

"What have you found out?" Karl asked quickly.

"Are our parents alive? Do we leave tonight?"

Johann threw up both hands in protest. "Boys, boys," he chided, "please give me time! First, Mama, it's so good to see you again. I hope you like the new dress material." He hugged her long and fiercely. "Now then, boys, I think you had better sit down and listen to what I have to tell you."

Oh-oh. Hearts sinking at the heaviness in Johann's words, they all sat down at what had now become their conference table. Greta brought coffee and Johann sat forward with his hands laced around the hot cup.

"Are my parents dead?" Karl asked dully.

Johann sighed raggedly. "I don't know about your father, Karl. Nor your sister. But your mother has been smuggled into Palestine and is working on a kibbutz helping to grow oranges and vegetables. The Red Cross could find no trace of Sonia, but they believe your father is in some concentration camp. They think the Germans may have kept him alive because he's a bricklayer." He sighed again. "I'm sorry I don't have better news, Karl, but at least your mother is safe."

Karl stared at the scuffed oilcloth covering the table. "Can I be with her?"

"That's the next step, once we get you into Switzerland. Some small boats posing as fishing boats are getting a number of people into Palestine."

Karl's smile was whimsical. "We Jews have a saying. 'Next year in Jerusalem.' " He nodded. "I'd like to go to my mother."

"We will pray for your father," Johann said. He laid a hand on Karl's arm. "If he makes it through this wretched war, you will see him again one day. Meanwhile, Franz, the news for you is a little better. Your parents served a year in prison and have just been released."

"They're free!" Franz whispered. His face radiated joy and unbelief and hope and fear. "Will I be allowed to go home?"

Johann's craggy face broke into a smile. "Those are the plans." He glanced at the big old clock, faithfully plucking off the minutes. "We leave tonight. Are you both ready?"

"Ach," Mrs. Hanssler broke in. "They have been ready since you were here before!"

"It's not going to be storming," Franz reminded Johann, and was humiliated when his voice cracked.

"True. But there is no moon either, so it will be very dark. When you get into Switzerland, you will see a village in front of you. Since the Swiss are not at war, it will be lighted. Walk straight forward and there will be a man signaling to you with a light. He will care for you until the Red Cross takes over." The man pulled out a folded paper and smoothed the creases on the table. "Now, then, you have work to do. You have about four hours to become familiar with this map so that we will make the least amount of noise possible as we travel after dark."

They ate a hurried supper later in the evening and after darkness enfolded the land, the trio was ready to go. Karl pressed the gold coins into Johann's palm and Franz picked up the battered rucksack.

Greta's faded blue eyes were shiny with tears as she pressed her rough hands against the faces of her boys and told them goodbye. "Be very careful," she whispered. "And remember, if ever you need to come back, you have a home here."

Both Franz and Karl felt deep emotions for this woman who had so unselfishly put her own life in danger to save them, and they wrapped their arms around the frail old shoulders.

Johann kissed his mother goodbye and the trio left the house and pressed quickly into the woods. It would be a long fourteen kilometers without a torch to light their way. They could speak only in whispers and then not unless it was an emergency. Even the snap of a twig could reveal their presence in the woods.

At times they must leave the trees and cross boggy areas, ditches and fields. Unsuspecting ditches were the hardest and sometimes one of the boys would trip and fall headlong. Other times they sank ankle deep in mud and their shoes made loud sucking noises when they pulled their feet free.

Ten kilometers left them chugging and panting but without having had any major problems. They had only four kilometers, or about two and a half miles to travel.

"We're going to make it," Franz whispered.

Johann stopped abruptly. "Shhh!"

Quickly he ducked behind a heavy stand of pine trees. Sensing some unknown danger, the boys pressed into the trees with him. Their flesh rose in goose bumps. Hearts pounding wildly, they waited. Not knowing. Not understanding.

Then they saw it. A pale fluttering light coming toward them. Voices sounded. Soldiers! Maybe the SS! Had they come so far only to be discovered now?

Johann grasped their wrists and began backtracking. One step at a time. Easy. Easy. A broken twig would sound like a pistol shot in the woods at night.

"The rocks!" Johann whispered. "Follow me."

Faintly, the boys recalled seeing a great clump of boulders on the map. But how could they make it to a safe place in the rocks on such a black and eerie night?

Feeling for every step, Johann led them upwards into the rocks. Then inch by inch he pulled them down into a kind of hollow that was ringed around by giant boulders. Crouching low, they waited for the soldiers to pass.

Yeshua. . . .

Jesus. . . .

Hide us well, Lord, Johann prayed.

The soldiers did not pass. Dropping exhausted on the very rocks where the trio hid, they drank from canteens and ate something that smelled like cabbage rolls. For twenty-five minutes they joked and talked before moving away. Franz was reluctant to come out of hiding, for he remembered all too well how the Hitler Youth had doubled back.

Every minute they hesitated was like an eternity, but Johann finally led them from the rocks and back through the woods. They crossed fields of stubble and then a meadow and another wooded area. At last they spotted the far off mist of lights.

Johann cupped his hands around his mouth and whispered, "Swiss village." He tugged at their sleeves. "Come. Slowly, slowly."

The sentry box showed up even blacker than the night around them. A lone sentry, bored and weary, waited silently. Johann cautioned the youths to remain where they were while he went forward alone. Hearing the sound of his approach, the sentry snapped to attention and lifted his rifle.

"*Hande hoch!*"

Johann obediently threw both hands into the air, and the boys could hear a murmured conversation. "Ja. Ja." A disgruntled, "Thank you," and Johann returned to motion the two youths forward.

He patted their shoulders, gave them a flashlight, and said, "Go. It is all right."

Still not completely sure of their fate, when they were three yards from the Swiss frontier, they broke into a dead run. They raced, zigzagging, until they had cleared the Swiss sentry as well.

A hundred yards from the village they stopped, gasping for breath. Their mouths were dry as a desert and their stomachs growled with hunger. A year of fear and running was behind them. They had crossed rivers, survived uncounted dangers, encountered nameless terrors, and yet God's hand of protection had never left them.

Now they were free. Laughing with nervous relief, they faced one another and solemnly shook hands. Then, squaring their shoulders and lifting their chins, they walked toward the village, where a man with a flashlight was signaling them.

Christian titles available from

PO Box 324
Somerville, IN 47683
(812) 795-2502
moorebooks@hotmail.com

Coming Soon: The Cathy and Carl series by Dorothy Grunbock Johnston, originally published in the 1950's. The first two titles will be published in January 2001 with the remaining titles published late summer of 2001.

Cathy and Carl of the Covered Wagon

The Callaway family is off to the Northwest country over the Oregon Trail with plenty of unexpected adventures for Cathy and Carl. The story will thrill girls as well as boys.

Cathy and Carl Captured

Oregon country at last and a winter at the Whitman's lone mission. There's unrest among the Indians and Cathy and Carl are whisked away by unfriendly Indians.

Cathy and Carl Join the Gold Rush   **Cathy and Carl Shipwrecked**
Cathy and Carl and the Sea Horse   **Cathy and Carl Ride the Pony Express**

Lost on the Trail   Kenneth N. Taylor   (8-12 yrs)   91 pages   **$6.50**

Pain, love, fear, hate, joy, hope, anxiety—these are some of the contrasting elements of drama in *Lost on the Trail*. The whole story revolves about intense rivalry between Bill Baker and Art Smith.

Bill is a serious boy, kind, considerate, and a Christian—though not a strong one. When an exciting and invigorating hike turns into a nightmare it is Bill who leads the staggering, exhausted group to safety. This episode makes him a hero, and the bitter enemy of Art.

Art Smith is a coward and a bully. Because of his cheating, lying, and stealing, the others turn against him and ostracize him. Hatred swells in his heart, resulting in a strenuous fight with God and Satan. This intense hatred develops into a cunning plot—a plot to get even with Bill.

In *Lost on the Trail*, Jesus Christ is the Good Shepherd who leads His lost ones home. He calms the fearful, comforts the sorrowful, and helps the desperate.

Run for your Life   Betty Swinford   (8-12 yrs)   108 pages   **$6.50**

Books by Craig and Louise Massey

The Stranger in the Marsh   (8-12 yrs)   93 Pages   **$6.50**

Sixteen-year-old Kerry Abbott had two loves: wildlife and photography. When he was asked to photograph all of the wildlife in Whispering Marsh, it was a dream come true. Three months of camping and taking pictures . . . what could be more fun?

He wasn't counting on rattlesnakes, however. Or loosing all of his food. Or the elusive Ben Faraway, who lived on an island in the Marsh.

And he certainly didn't expect to find himself a prisoner in a cave. . . .

Join Kerry as he encounters The Stranger in the Marsh!

Twig the Collie   (8-12 yrs)   101 pages   **$6.50**

Fifteen-year-old Gordon Hart is being punished for a crime he didn't commit. Gordon is convinced that no one will ever believe him, and gives up trying to prove his innocence. One day, however, he meets Johnny Blueweather, who **does** believe his story. Johnny's friendship comes to mean even more to Gordon than Twig, his beautiful collie. Johnny's greatest gift to Gordon, though, was when he introduced him to Someone Else who took the punishment for another. . . .

Indian Drums and Broken Arrows   (10-14 yrs)   136 pages   **$6.99**

The Revolutionary War. Jeff Lockwood's father had defected to the redcoats. Or so it was rumored. Was it true? Jeff had to find out, in spite of the danger.

An Indian attack. A girl held prisoner. Jeff's heroic rescue. Each exciting element adds to the suspense of this prize winning novel of conflict and espionage.

Brown Shadow   (10-14 yrs)   136 pages   **$6.99**

Jeff saves an abandoned Indian boy, Brown Shadow, from starvation. Then he must face the hatred and prejudice of the settlers.

A helpless Indian boy. An angry mob. Jeff and Brown Shadow's narrow escapes from the hangman's noose and a burning building. Each element makes this an exciting sequel to **Indian Drums and Broken Arrows**.

Captain Daley's Missing Houseboat   (8-12 yrs)   68 pages   **$3.50**

When Captain Daley retired and moved to Shadyville to be near his daughter, he thought his days of adventure were over. He sure missed the boat with that idea.

To begin with, Noah's Ark, the Captain's houseboat, becomes a sort of clubhouse for four boy detectives—that is, until someone steals it! Who would want Noah's Ark, and why?

Then the Captain himself disappears, and it's up to the Crew to find him.

Captain Daley's Crew in Danger   (8-12 yrs)   64 pages   **$3.50**

Captain Daley and Crew are back in another exciting adventure!

The note from the Captain read: "I have a wonderful surprise for my Sunday school class. It may mean a very exciting adventure for all of you." When Pudge, Slim, and the rest of us each received a copy of the note, we were excited! It had been a while since we solved the mystery of The Missing Houseboat, and we were ready for anything—or so we thought.

Helping the Captain's friend Bob finish his Log Cabin Church sounded so easy, even though we knew there we those who would stop at nothing to keep the church from opening. But that was before the threats, and the mysterious midnight visitor. . .

Captain Daley's Crew and the Peg-Legged Tramp (8-12 yrs)   80 pages **$3.50**

An abandoned grist mill and its peg-legged dweller involve Gary and his pals in a mystery that goes back into the past. They find the buried spoils of a long-forgotten jewel robbery, and their attempts to solve the mystery lead to some surprising developments. The adventure is further complicated with the entry of Jill, a girl from a neighboring farm. In the end the young folks learn that God works in mysterious ways His wonders to perform.

Captain Daley's Crew at Thunderhead Lake   (8-12 yrs)   80 pages   **$3.50**
When the Captain and his young Crew take a houseboat cruise up Big Bear River to Thunderhead Lake, they encounter one surprising development after another. Mysterious explosions—a red airplane that shouldn't be there—a strange bearded man scurrying through the woods at night—all combine to give the boys some never-to-be-forgotten thrills. They enjoy an even greater thrill when they lead a backwoods boy to Christ.

Captain Daley's Crew and the Long-Eared Taxicab   (8-12 yrs) 56 pages   **$3.50**
When Captain Daley and crew go to spend a few weeks at Wonderlost Lake, Pudge discovers he can earn a little extra income with his donkey, which he calls "The Long Eared Taxicab." They're also kept busy assisting Professor Jamieson, and ornithologist, who is recording the different varieties of bird calls in the area for research.
Mr. Quoggins, a strange little man who visits Wonderlost Lake every year, hires Pudge's "Taxicab". He's been looking for something . . . what is it? And then Professor Jamieson's daughter, Jennifer, runs away. Can the Crew find her? More importantly, will the Jamiesons listen to the Crew when they tell them about the One who can make a difference in their home?

Captain Daley's Crew and the Jungle Ship   (8-12 yrs)   68 pages   **$3.50**
Adventure is no stranger to Captain Daley's Crew, but it had never come on the heels of a hurricane before! The ship "The Merry Breeze" is marooned on Ghost Island because of the storm, and the captain of the ship quickly enlists the help of Captain Daley and the Crew.
The Crew soon learns that the ship is full of wild animals from the jungles of Africa, and the animals are all hungry, because their food was ruined in the storm. As Captain Daley and the Crew round up food and supplies for the animals and passengers, they begin to realize that something isn't quite right about the jungle ship. Why is the crew of the "Merry Breeze" threatening to abandon the ship? Why is Captain Lunninger so evasive about their destination? And who is the mysterious African boy Captain Lunninger keeps on board?

Please contact us for a catalog.

Moore Books
PO Box 324
Somerville, IN 47683
(812) 795-2502
moorebooks@hotmail.com

Prices subject to change without notice.
Indiana residents add 5% sales tax.
    Add $3.00 Shipping & Handling for orders $30.00 or less. Shipping and Handling for orders more than $30.00 add 10%.